THE LEGACY

By

MARGARET D. CLARK

New Generation Publishing

THE LEGACY

YOU DON'T HAVE TO BELIEVE IN GHOSTS
TO SEE ONE

ALSO BY THE AUTHOR

THE MAGIC KINGDOM

The author has seen ghosts, auras and had visions all her life. It has taught her that life is eternal and love never dies.

CHAPTER ONE

THE LEGACY

The manor house stood alone and at the end of a long row of hotels and smaller type guest houses all silent, dark and empty for the time of year. The sea could be heard in the distance, pounding against the rocks.

'This can't be right, Charlie,' cried Meg.

'Well. I don't know where else it can be,' he muttered, looking around. 'Let's have a look at the map again.'

She quickly pulled it out of her rucksack. The two teenagers poured over the map their heads close together. Meg's dark auburn hair was cut in a short bob framing her elfin features and striking green eyes. It was a contrast to, Charlie's dark brown eyes, wavy black hair and handsome good looks that could steal any girl's heart.

'We're in the right place,' he said.

They both looked up.

'That's our legacy,' she cried, with a look of astonishment.

'Wow,' said Charlie.

They stared in amazement.

'Well, what are we dithering about here for, let's take a walk.'

Meg stuffed the map back into her rucksack and they set off along the wide neglected driveway. They hadn't gone far before, Meg had the feeling someone was watching their every move. She looked over her shoulder, but there was no one there. The ghostly atmosphere made her suddenly fearful. She turned to, Charlie to say something and changed her mind. She couldn't face another argument.

The manor house stood before them in isolated splendour in its tranquil setting. The solid oak door had a round door knob and above it was a stained glass window. It showed a picture of a sailing ship from a bygone age in full colour, set jauntily on a wild and windswept sea. The windows on either side were large and spacious, the brickwork was in a good state of repair and there was an air of mystery about it.

'Wow, this is awesome,' he said.

'Oh, Charlie isn't it wonderful. I can't wait to see inside.'

'You've got the keys.'

Meg fumbled about in her rucksack and quickly brought out the keys. She was trembling with excitement and almost dropped them.

'You're in a worse state than I am,' admitted Charlie, and before they had time to insert the key, the door swung open. They exchanged a startled glance before stepping over the thresh hold.

'HELLO,' called out, Charlie into the silence. 'Is anyone there?' But there was no reply.

They both jumped with fright when the door slammed shut behind them. The house was empty and nobody lived there. A clock chimed the hour of six its echoes rang eerily through the house.

Charlie located the light switch and turned on the light, chasing away the dark shadows of early evening. 'That's better,' he said, gazing about him.

Meg was still clinging on to his arm as they paused to look around. She could see mouse droppings in one corner of the room and cobwebs were hanging from the ceiling, and a strange aroma filled the air.

'What's that awful pong?' said Charlie.

'It's the scent of lilacs,' said Meg, with a stunned look. 'It was Aunty Nell's favourite perfume.' And a creepy feeling washed over her.

Charlie gave her an odd look.

It soon faded away.

They gazed about them in wonder. The wide hallway was elegant and spacious, leading up to a broad staircase. A crystal chandelier dangled from the ceiling giving it an air of nobility. They walked from room to room. The paintwork was shabby and the wallpaper was faded in places. Thick red carpet covered the floor everywhere they looked, and luxurious ruby red curtains were hanging from dirty windows. The rooms were well furnished and there was a musty smell in all the rooms.

The first thing they saw as they entered the dining room was the painting hanging on the far wall. They went over for a closer look. It showed the manor house in all its splendour, as it had once been a long time ago. The extensive grounds were well turned out. The lord of the manor stood proudly to one side. He was tall and handsome with a rakish look about him. His dark bewitching eyes seemed to follow their every move. The artist had given great attention to detail. It was cleverly done.

'What a beautiful painting,' said Meg.

'Wow, it's an original,' cried Charlie in astonishment. 'Look, Meg the artist's name is there in the bottom right hand corner.'

'So it is, Gabriel Scott,' she said.

'He must have stayed here at one time,' said Charlie, thoughtfully.

'Well, we'll never know.' And a strange feeling washed over her.

They stood admiring it for a moment longer before moving on. They wandered into a kitchen. Shiny pots and pans and cooking utensils were hanging in neat little rows from hooks in the wall. A teacloth was draped untidily over a kitchen stool, and a row of freshly washed pots sat on the draining board. There was not a speck of dust anywhere.

'How odd, someone's been in here, Charlie'

'Well, they're not here now,' he said, dismissively. 'You'll have to learn to cook now, Meg,' he added with a cheeky grin.

'Oh, Charlie, I'm not that bad.'

He rolled his eyes at her and it set them both off laughing.

'Let's see what's in here,' said Charlie, going into the next room.

Meg followed him in.

It was a well furnished sitting room with plain white washed walls. It had a peaceful air about it as if the owner was due back at any moment. They could see it had been the owner's private quarters.

'This is cosy,' she said, looking idly around.

'We'll make it our own,' he said, smiling.

They shook off their rucksacks and put them down.

Meg had the feeling of being watched. 'I feel like we're being spied on, Charlie,' she whispered.

'There's no one else here, but us,' stated Charlie, with a firm look before, drifting away into the next room.

Meg hurried in after him. The room was poorly lit after turning on the light and left dark corners in the room.

It was a well furnished bedroom. A large dust sheet covered the big four poster bed. A small faded photograph in a silver frame sat on the window sill. Meg went over to it and was surprised to see it was a black and white photograph taken ten years ago. It showed her, Mum and Aunty Nell in their younger days. They each held the hand of a small child between them and they were all smiling brightly. The sea view was in the background.

Meg picked it up for a closer look. 'Come and see this, Charlie.'

'What is it, Meg?' He quickly joined her.

She pointed with her forefinger. 'This photo must have been taken when I was about six years old. That's mum, there's Aunty Nell and that's me in the middle.'

'Why did you never keep in touch?'

Meg was thoughtful. 'I'd forgotten about her,' she said. 'But I can still remember, Mum and Aunty Nell having a blazing row and Aunty Nell left in tears. She never came to see us again.'

'Families should stick together through thick and thin,' cried Charlie in disgust, before wandering off.

Meg was left gazing at the holiday snap with a faraway look on her face, as memories came flooding in of happy times gone by. The ache in her heart of losing her family never left her, and it never would. She gave a sigh of such longing, before placing it back on the window sill. She turned around and saw the ghost of a pirate standing in the shadows watching her. He was a fearsome sight.

The colour drained from her face in fright and she was slowly sliding down the wall when, Charlie appeared with a big smile on his face it quickly changed to one of concern when he saw the change in her.

He dashed to her side. 'Meg, Meg,' he cried. 'Are you ill?' His arms went around her and she leaned against him. 'Come and sit down,' he said, gently guiding her into a chair.

She fell into it.

He looked worriedly at her.

'Oh, Charlie, I've just seen a g-ghost.' She just blurted it all out.

'I don't believe in all that rubbish,' he cried. 'How many times do I have to tell you, there's no such things as ghosts.'

There was a mutinous look about her.

'Look, Meg we're both worn out after such a long journey to get here. So let's eat our sandwiches and drink the rest of our coffee and think about where we're going to sleep tonight.'

'We've haven't been upstairs, yet, Charlie.'

'We'll leave it till morning it's too dark to get a proper look, anyway.

Meg was quick to agree. She gave a small shiver as an icy chill filled the room. 'It's freezing in here, Charlie.'

'I'll light the fire.' Charlie struck a match from the small box of matches he always carried with him. The gas fired flared into life sending warmth around the room.

'The solicitor kept his word when he said, he would see to things for us,' he commented. 'Can you imagine what it would have been like to be fumbling around this place in the dark?'

She just grimaced.

The room was soon warm and cosy. They took off their winter coats and draped them untidily over two chairs. They made themselves comfortable and began to eat their leftover sandwiches. They chatted about their legacy and the strange circumstances they found themselves in.

Ω

The manor house had been left to Meg by her, Aunty Nell and any of her surviving relatives which now included Charlie since they were married. Meg had been difficult to find, as she had left no forwarding address and had changed her maiden name of, Simpson to her married name of, Moffett when she married Charlie. Several long months had passed before her whereabouts were discovered, and it had been a difficult case.

They had both worked for the same firm. Charlie had worked as a joiner and, Meg had left college and taken a job as a junior typist in the typing pool. Love had blossomed when their paths crossed on a regular basis. Marriage had not been discussed as they were both still teenagers enjoying their time together.

The unexpected death of Meg's parents in a road accident had changed everything. Meg's parents had made no provision for her, assuming they would live to a ripe old age. The house she had lived in all her life had been mortgaged to the hilt. It was quickly sold to pay funeral expenses and other outstanding bills.

Meg at sixteen years old was homeless. She had been invited to stay at a friend's already busy household, as a temporary measure. Charlie lived in a tiny flat and there was no room for Meg, and he knew the landlord wouldn't allow it. They were deeply in love.

Charlie had vowed to love her forever. They had the consent and approval of her, Aunt Nell's long term friend and solicitor as acting guardian until she was older. He had vetted, Charlie closely and could see they were deeply in love and that he would look after his young charge. And in the short time he had known them he had become fond of them both.

Ω

It was a quiet wedding. Meg looked beautiful in a stunning white wedding gown, and wore a tiara of small pink rosebuds over her auburn hair that shone like spun gold. Charlie was very smart in a new suit and his hair was brushed back from a wide intelligent forehead. They were married in the small church nearby with a few friends in attendance.

Charlie and Meg had rented a furnished apartment on the edge of town with views overlooking a park. They were very happy for eight wonderful months. Then disaster struck when the firm they both worked for went bankrupt. The same week, the landlord doubled the rent of their apartment making it impossible for them to stay there. Their savings were quickly dwindling away and they were in a desperate situation.

The legacy and the grand sum of seven hundred and fifty pounds had arrived, just in the nick of time to save them from becoming homeless. They'd packed all they owned into two rucksacks and said farewell to their friends, promising to keep in touch. And set off into the unknown on the greatest adventure of their young lives.

Ω

'Let's check out the bed,' she said, jumping up.
'Okay,' he said with a cheeky grin.
They went into the bedroom.
'I suppose this will have to do,' she said, gazing at the

four poster bed covered in a dust sheet. It was quickly thrown off to reveal a brand new mattress complete with the label still attached in case there was any doubt.

'Oh, Charlie look, it's a new bed.'

'The solicitor has seen to everything,' remarked Charlie. 'Just like he said he would.'

'I must write and thank him. Now let's see if we can find some nice clean bedding,' said Meg, looking around. She opened a large cupboard built discreetly along one wall everything they needed was in there. They got to work and the bed was soon nicely made with clean laundered bedding, still smelling faintly of some soapy fabric.

Charlie returned to the cosy sitting room turning everything off leaving the room in darkness before returning to, Meg with their rucksacks. They quickly undressed and climbed into bed.

'Did you hear that,' she whispered.

'No, I didn't hear anything.'

They cuddled up together and were soon fast asleep.

CHAPTER TWO

A STRANGE MEETING

Charlie and Meg were both up early after a good night's sleep. The chilly morning air seemed to fill the house giving it a damp and unloved feeling, but nothing could dampen their high spirits. They were as happy as skylarks.

'Oh, Charlie, I can't believe this is our home.'

'It's smashing isn't it?'

'Wonderful.'

They couldn't stop smiling.

'I don't know about you, but I'm starving. 'Let's go and grab a bite to eat before we do anything else,' suggested Charlie. 'We can have a good look around when we get back.'

'Food always comes first with you,' she said, laughing. 'But I am hungry,' she admitted.

They wasted no time in leaving.

The seaside resort of, Salt Water Bay with its scattering off shops, bingo halls, amusement arcades and chip shops was quiet, Charlie and Meg were in the holiday making industry, but it was still early in the year and few people were about. They soon spotted a cafe sign and stepped inside the, TEAPOT CAFE. The delicious aroma of bacon and eggs frying assailed their nostrils, it made them realise how hungry they were. There were only a few hardy souls in the cafe and they chose a table near the window. The waitress hurried over to take their order. They didn't have long to wait before she returned with two huge breakfasts, which she placed on the table in front of them.

'Enjoy your meal,' she said, pleasantly and whirled away to serve the next customer.

Charlie and Meg enjoyed their breakfast cooked to perfection, then looked casually around as they drank their tea. A mature lady was sitting at the next table and caught, Meg's eye and she gave her a smile inviting a response.

'You're new here, aren't you?' said the stranger. Mousy brown hair sprinkled with a few grey strands framed an intelligent face and, blue eyes as sharp as a knife looked out from behind rimless glasses. She was petite and warmly dressed against the cold weather.

'We only arrived yesterday,' said Meg, smiling. Do you live here, too?'

'Yes, but only until the end of the week, then I must find somewhere else to live or I'll be out on the street.'

Meg frowned at her.

'That doesn't give you much time to find somewhere,' said Charlie, startled.

'My landlord has put the rent up and I can't possibly pay what he asks so I will have to move out.' She gave a huge sigh. 'My life hasn't been the same since, my best friend died suddenly of a heart attack. But I really shouldn't trouble you with my problems.' Her face was creased with worry. Meg realised the older woman would have been about the same age as her own dear mum, had she still been alive.

'Why not come and stay with us, we have plenty of room,' offered Meg, impulsively. Charlie looked taken aback then quickly agreed.

'Oh, my dear, what a wonderful offer, but I couldn't possibly impose on you, after all you are both strangers to me but very nice strangers,' she added, quickly.

'Well, at least come and see the place before you decide,' suggested Charlie.

'I'll come with you on one condition,' she paused. 'And that you allow me to buy your breakfast.'

'Okay,' said Meg, lightly. She understood the need to pay back a kindness.

'You don't have to do that,' cried Charlie. 'We can get our own.'

'Oh, I insist,' she said. 'Otherwise, I'm sorry to say, I couldn't impose on your generosity.' She got up to leave.

Meg prodded him in the ribs and he suddenly had a change of heart.

'That would be very nice,' said Charlie, and added. 'Thank you,' and gave her a winsome smile.

She gave him a shrewd look.

The bill was paid and they left the cafe together.

'Shall we introduce ourselves?'

'My name is Charlie Moffett and this is my lovely wife, Meg and we are very pleased to meet you,' said Charlie giving her a sweeping bow.

They all laughed together.

'My name is Pearl Robinson.'

They set off in friendly fashion.

Meg suddenly stopped to look in a grocery shop window they were about to pass. 'Let's go in,' she said.

They went in and looked around. They did a quick shop and left. Pearl had insisted on buying them a box of chocolate biscuits which she carried in a small bag. They walked briskly along until they came to the entrance to their new home.

'We're here,' he said.

'This is our home, now,' announced Meg, proudly.

'B-but this was Nell's house,' cried Pearl.

'You knew, Aunt Nell,' cried Meg.

'Oh, yes,' she cried. 'Nell was my dear friend and it was, Nell I was talking about when I said my best friend had died.'

They were all taken aback for a moment.

'Well, in that case, we'll have loads to talk about,' said Meg, and glanced at Charlie.

'I can't wait to hear it,' he said, dryly.

Pearl walked between them down the well remembered driveway in a daze. Once inside they went straight to the cosy sitting room they had decided to make their own, situated at the back of the manor house and overlooking the huge gardens.

'It's so lovely being back here again,' said Pearl, looking around. 'This was Nell's sitting room, you know.'

'Will it upset you to talk about her,' Meg asked. 'I would like to know what she was like. I was only a child when she left our home after a family row, and I never saw her again,' she admitted. 'And I never did find out what the row was all about.'

Pearl looked pensive for a moment. 'I can answer that,' she said. 'Your mum thought, Nell was turning you into a spoilt little madam, because she couldn't say no to you and your childish demands.'

Meg was amazed. 'Is that all,' she said.

'I'm afraid so, but raking up the past never does any good. However, I can tell you what a wonderful person, Nell was.'

'I would like that, but shall we have tea first?' enquired Meg.

'That would be nice. There's nothing like a cup of tea to warm you up on a cold day.'

Meg smiled at her before trotting off into the kitchen.

Charlie had lit the fire during the exchange. He turned to Pearl. 'It'll soon warm up now. Why not take off your coat and sit down,' suggested Charlie, politely pulling out a chair from beneath the table. Pearl shrugged off her winter coat and placed it over the back of a chair before taking the seat Charlie offered.

Meg returned with the tea things on a small tray she had found in the kitchen and placed it on the table before taking a seat between, Pearl and Charlie. The chocolate biscuits were opened and handed around. Meg and Pearl were soon in deep conversation. Charlie felt left out of things and decided to go for a walk. He pushed his chair back and stood up.

They both glanced up at him.

'I'm going outside for a quick look around.' He gave a sudden grin. 'I'm sure you can both manage without me. And off he went.'

They were both smiling as he left the room.

12

'That's a nice young man you have there,' remarked Pearl.

CHAPTER THREE

THE SEASHORE

Charlie set off with a spring in his step and headed for the cliff tops and vast expanse of ocean. He walked briskly along until he reached the harbour filled with little boats and, yachts bobbing about on the tranquil water that lapped at the sides with a gentle rhythm. A cool refreshing breeze caressed the seashore and it had a soothing effect on him as he headed for the beach and soft golden sands. Then on a sudden impulse took off his trainers and socks, tucked them well into his trainers and left them neatly on the beach beside a low stone wall. He rolled the bottom of his jeans up to his knees and went for a paddle. The brazing cold water made him gasp and laugh out loud, as he waded in with all the excitement of a child as the cold water lapped around his ankles. Seagulls flew wildly overhead flapping their wings, screeching loudly and foraging for food.

Charlie loved the sea and wondered if he came from a long line of ancient mariners. His parents were a mystery to him as he had lived in various children's homes all his life, and had suffered the loneliness of never truly belonging anywhere or to anyone. He'd run away on his fourteenth birthday to make his own way in the world and, because he looked older than his fourteen years had found work. Meg was the best thing that had ever happened to him and he loved her dearly.

He gave a last glance out to sea and along the shoreline there was not a soul about, before turning away to walk back to where he had left his trainers. He sat on the low stone wall and dried his feet on his socks, before putting his trainers back on. He stuffed his damp sandy socks into his pockets, shook the legs of his jeans down and, with a carefree air headed for home.

The manor house was the most beautiful thing he had ever seen, even in its neglected state it had taken his breath away, and he had instantly fallen in love with it. He smiled secretly to himself and a solitary dog walker passing by smiled back. He set off jauntily for home with a song in his heart and whistling a jolly sea shanty.

CHAPTER FOUR

EVERYTHING HAPPENS FOR A REASON

'I knew Nell all my life. She was a lovely person with a heart of gold. We worked in the same office together doing secretarial work, and every Saturday night we used to get dolled up and go dancing in the local dance hall. It's where we met our husbands.' She smiled softly to herself. 'I married my, Tom shortly after, Nell married Reginald Mortimer. She always called him her dear, Reggie. He was a racing driver, you know.'

'What happened to him?'

'He died, of a fatal heart attack, just dropped down dead in front of her. She was never the same after that.'

'Life sucks,' said Meg, quietly.

Pearl gave her a surprised look then carried on. 'When Nell discovered her beloved, Reggie had spent all their savings. She was heartbroken, as she couldn't afford the upkeep of a house this size. Reggie had bought her the manor house as a wedding present out of his race winnings and she didn't want to live anywhere else. Somehow word must have got out that money was tight and along came a rogue who claimed he was one of Reggie's racing colleagues. He said he felt duty bound to help his widow out and offered to buy the manor house seeing that she could no longer afford to keep it. He had a sly way about him, and offered a ridiculously low price. Nell told him firmly she would never sell the manor house, under any circumstances, but he wouldn't take no for an answer and kept popping up with a higher offer each time. She ended up chasing him off the premises with a pitchfork, in the end. He thought he could wear her down but he was no match for Nell.' A little chuckle escaped her.

It made, Meg smile.

Pearl took a deep breath and carried on. 'Then Nell had this absolute brainwave of turning the manor house into a hotel for summer visitors it would give her an income, so she wouldn't have to sell it.' Pearl chuckled as she re-lived the moment. 'It was a wonderful idea as it has ten bedrooms with two more on the ground floor,' she paused for a moment. 'There used to be access to a private beach well, more of a cove really it used to be called smugglers cove, but the cove has long since gone due to a landslide as cliffs have eroded away over time. It's not safe in places, but there are still some nice walks along the cliff tops with stunning sea views.

'We haven't had chance to look around anywhere, yet,' explained Meg. 'We wanted to get something to eat first and that's how we ended up in the cafe, or we would never have met.'

They both smiled.

'I was delighted when, Nell asked me to join her. She wanted us to be partners, but I didn't want that and said I was quite happy just to help. She said I would have to live on the premises if we were to succeed, and I couldn't wait to move out of my tiny flat, no bigger than a broom cupboard, really. Nell gave me one of the loveliest rooms on the ground floor overlooking the beautiful gardens. Our husbands died around the same time so, Nell and I grieved together. We were never lucky enough to have children,' she said, softly. 'Just never meant to be, I suppose.'

'You'd have made a great mum.'

'Why, thank you, my dear.'

'Was it a success?'

'Oh, yes, my dear, it was a little gold mine once we got started. We were so busy we couldn't fit everyone in and had to turn people away. We were rushed off our feet for six solid months of the year. We made enough money in one summer season to pay all the bills and, still had plenty left over to spend the winter in a tropical paradise. We spent the coldest part of the year sunbathing and even went on a few cruises. We always came back refreshed and ready to start work again. They were wonderful times.'

Meg's mouth dropped open in astonishment.

'Oh, don't get me wrong it was hard work at first, and at times we felt like tearing our hair out, but it helped us get through the grief of losing our husbands, and we soon got the hang of it and were actually beginning to enjoy ourselves. But I've left out the most important part.' She paused. 'Before we could put our plan into action, we needed a handy man to do all the odd jobs that required attention before we could open as a hotel. Then one day, someone came knocking on the door. It took us both by surprise as we weren't expecting visitors. We opened the door to a dirty looking tramp. He had a wild look about him and was as thin as a stick. We thought he was going to attack us when he suddenly lurched forward, before collapsing on the doorstep. We thought, at first, he was dead, but he soon came round. He begged us for a drink of water and a bite to eat. We were horrified at the state he was in and knew he meant us no harm.'

Meg gasped in horror. 'What did you do?'

'Fed him, of course, Nell had him sitting up at the table with a decent meal in front of him, quick as a flash. It was all washed down with enough tea to sink a battleship. When he'd finished eating, he folded his knife and fork neatly on the plate, looked over at us and suddenly burst into heartbreaking tears, great wracking sobs shook his poor emaciated body. It was terrible to see and we were both so shocked we didn't know what to say to him. Nell didn't hesitate and took him in her arms to comfort him until the storm was over.'

'What a lovely thing to do.'

'She was like that. He was only a young man and it was much later when he told us it had been his birthday the day he arrived, and we had saved his life as he had been thinking of ending it all. He was only nineteen years old.'

'Oh, how awful,' said Meg deeply moved.

'I remember how embarrassed he was for breaking down like that. He couldn't apologise enough then he asked if there was any work he could do in return for all our kindness. He spoke in cultured tones that surprised us both and told us his name was, Gabriel Scott.' Pearl suddenly smiled. 'Nell wasn't one to miss an opportunity and told him we desperately needed a handy man about the place for all the minor repairs requiring attention. She told him of our plan to open as a hotel for the summer season as soon as all the work had been done. She offered him somewhere to sleep and all the food he could eat. She said he would be doing us a favour if he could do the work for us, as we had no money. I remember his look of suspicion and convinced him it was true and it wasn't charity, but necessity and we truly had no money to pay anyone and a deal was struck.'

'Were things really that bad?'

'We were as poor as church mice. We couldn't even afford to buy a new hat. Nell gave Gabriel a room at the back of the house that looked out onto a small patio with glass doors which opened out onto the garden. She also gave him some of, Reggie's old clothes that she had kept hidden away. We hardly recognised him when he was smartened up. Gabriel was the best handy man anyone could wish for.'

'That was a stroke of luck, then,' said Meg.

'Most fortunate,' agreed Pearl. 'He fixed the boiler that was always breaking down and did a thousand and one other jobs that we were grateful for. Then one day he told us there was nothing left for him to do and it was time he left. He said he would never forget our kindness to him and presented us with a painting he'd done of the manor house. I expect you've seen it hanging in the dining room. I think that was when we realised he was a talented artist. We had grown very fond of, Gabriel and were sorry to see him leave. We never saw him again.' She gazed into the distance. 'Pride's a funny thing and Nell understood that.'

'How did my aunt die?'

'She died suddenly of a heart attack.' Pearl paused a moment as all the old feelings of loss swamped her, she quickly pulled herself together. 'We were as close as sisters, you know and I will always miss having her around.'

'The pain never leaves you,' said Meg.

Pearl waited for her to speak.

'My parents were killed in a car accident when I was only sixteen.' She went on to explain in a very subdued voice full of pain. 'They were coming home when their car skidded on an icy patch and they went into a deep ravine. They both died instantly.'

'Oh, my dear, how absolutely ghastly for you.' cried Pearl, with a look of horror.

'I didn't know what to do or where to go. I was an only child and had no family to turn to and only, Charlie was there for me and I don't know what I would have done without him. He was marvellous, and still is.' She added, softy.

'I was very surprised when he said you were married.' You both seem so young.'

'We belong together.' It was said with such conviction. 'Uncle Theo was the only other person that I could have turned to but he was away working at the time.' She went on to explain. 'Theo was an old friend of the family and an actor on stage and in films. He was a regular visitor to our home, dad used to jokingly call him mum's secret lover as, Theo would have married mum if dad, hadn't married her first. I wrote and told him about the accident and the funeral arrangements. He turned up on the day of the funeral and he looked a broken man.' Meg looked upset as she remembered it all so clearly.

Pearl could see how raw and painful it still was.

'I keep in touch with Uncle Theo by letter and I sent him an invite to my wedding, but he was away at the time filming, and knew nothing about it until much later. He sent us a cheque for one hundred pounds and promised to pay us a visit. He's the nearest thing I have to family now, so I asked if he would mind if I called him, Uncle Theo and he was delighted as he had no family either.'

'That would be a blessing for him,' said Pearl, deeply moved by all she had been told. 'I expect, Charlie's family were a great comfort to you.'

'Charlie's parents died shortly after he was born and he was taken into care. He knows nothing at all about them, or where he comes from. He's been looking after himself ever since he was fourteen and he's seventeen now.'

'You've had a rough time of it, my dear.'

They sat quietly together for a moment.

'I remember, Nell once telling me, she wanted to leave the manor house to her niece and, gave me details of her solicitor. I remember thinking at the time, it was as if she knew, she didn't have long to live, because she died a few weeks later.' Pearl sighed deeply before continuing. 'Nell knew I couldn't stay here, without her around, and I had enough money to live on so I moved out into a slightly bigger broom cupboard, and now I have less than a week before I move out and find somewhere else to live,' she said, worriedly.

CHAPTER FIVE

STRANGE TIMES

'I know what that feels like,' confessed Meg. 'Because that happened to us when we both lost our jobs when the firm we worked for went bust. We were both very frightened at the time, although, Charlie would never admit it.' She suddenly smiled and her face lit up. 'You could have knocked us down with a feather when a solicitor contacted us with the news that, Aunty Nell had died and left us her house and seven hundred and fifty pounds.'

Pearl gave her a wide smile. 'It was what she wanted, my dear.'

'I had forgotten all about her and felt terribly guilty at the time,' admitted Meg. 'Because I hadn't seen her in a very long time, as you know.'

'Such a waste,' said Pearl.

'The legacy saved us from becoming homeless. We could hardly believe it. We had somewhere to live and it was ours, but we had no idea it was a huge manor house with gardens the size of a football field.'

And they laughed quietly together.

'We still have the seven hundred and fifty pounds that Aunty Nell left us, plus fifty pounds of our own money. It's not much is it?' A feeling of panic set in. 'We must both find jobs very soon.'

'Why not carry on where, Nell and I left off and turn the manor house back into a prosperous hotel again.'

'What!' She cried. 'We can't do that we wouldn't know where to start.'

'I do.'

It hit them both at the same time.

'I'll help you get started, if you like,' offered Pearl.

'Do you really mean it,' asked Meg, incredulously.

'Of course, I mean it.' Pearl looked at the young woman she had grown to like immensely and reminded her so much of, Nell.

'Okay,' said Meg after a slight pause. 'It's a deal.'

They both burst out laughing. Suddenly Meg felt as if a great weight had been lifted from her young shoulders and it was all because of, Pearl's amazing offer.

'Let's get down to brass tacks then, shall we?' said Pearl. 'Will you be doing the cooking, my dear?'

'Oh, no,' she cried. 'I'm a hopeless cook.'

'Then the first thing we need to do is hire a cook.' She paused to look at, Meg. 'I'm sure we can manage the waitressing between us, and I'll teach you how to do the ordering and keep the books in order for the tax man. Oh, and we'll need some insurance. The rooms are usually given a quick tidy up after breakfast when the guests are out. Saturday morning is the busiest day with change over as new people arrive and others leave. Oh, and the naughty one nighters have to be watched in case they try to leave without paying their bill, and that can happen and we must advertise as soon as possible and the table seating arrangement for the guests must be done before anyone arrives.'

'What do you mean by seating arrangement? Doesn't everyone just sit down at a table for their meals?'

'Oh, no, my dear, the seating arrangement has to be planned ahead, or chaos will result.'

Meg gave her a puzzled look.

'Let me explain, everyone must know where to sit.' Pearl gave a girlish giggle. 'We once had a honeymoon couple in and we sat them on separate tables with complete strangers, due to an error, but they saw the funny side of it and we quickly changed things around so they could sit together. We laughed so much in those days trying to get things right.'

'It was fun though, wasn't it?'

'Not all the time,' she chuckled. 'There was a time when the delivery man forgot our order and, Nell had to go and collect it in the car, which reminds me, does Charlie drive?'

'Yes, he loves driving. He had a car, but sold it when he couldn't afford to run it anymore.'

'Oh, good, you'll need transport to get about and there's a car in the garage that he can use. Oh, and you had better get some business cards printed to let everyone know you are open for business, and the phone will have to be put back on and...'

'Oh, please stop,' cried Meg as her head began to swim. 'It's too much for me to take in all at once,' and she exploded into laughter.

Pearl soon joined in and, a strange bond of friendship had begun.

'I suppose it is a lot to take in all at once, and I have gone on a bit,' admitted Pearl, once they had calmed down. 'We called it, The Manor Hotel, it's got quite a nice ring to it don't you think so?'

'Yes, I like it. I can hardly believe this is all happening, but we'd be hopeless without your help, when can you move in?'

Now it was Pearl's turn to look astonished. 'Oh, my dear,' she cried. 'Are you sure?' She was suddenly overwhelmed as it dawned on her too, all the changes that were about to take please. 'But don't you want to speak to Charlie, first.'

'No I don't. Charlie will agree with me, in fact, he'll be over the moon when I tell him what we have planned.'

'Well, in that case, I can move in right away, but still have a word with Charlie, won't you, if only to set my mind at rest, I would hate to throw a spanner in the works.'

They heard footsteps coming towards them and looked up to see Charlie enter the room. They both smiled sweetly at him. He gave them a suspicious look and had the feeling they were hiding something from him.

'It's time I was leaving,' said Pearl, getting up and reaching for her winter coat lying over the back of a chair. She quickly put it on and fastened the buttons that ran down the front. 'I'll see you later.' She suddenly reached up and kissed, Charlie on the cheek as she passed. 'My knight in shining armour, and don't bother to see me out,' she cried, laughing. 'I know the way.'

Charlie watched her leave with a look of wonder. 'What have you been up to, Meg?' he asked, shrewdly.

'Oh, Charlie, I have the most wonderful news to tell you.'

He looked at his little angel. 'Let's hear it then.'

'How would you like to be manager of a hotel?'

'Tell me more?'

Meg filled him in on all the details. 'And Pearl has agreed to help us.'

They both looked stunned at the speed in which everything seemed to be happening.

'And you'll never guess, what, Charlie. There's an old car in the garage we can use,' she smiled at the look of delight that spread across his boyish good looks. 'And there's something else I haven't told you. I hope you don't mind, but I've invited Pearl to move in with us.'

'No, of course I don't mind, you silly goose, we'll need Pearl's help to make a success of it, and I couldn't bear to think of her on her own with nowhere to live, and I'll tell you something else,' he said. 'I was just about to ask you if she could stay with us, but you've beaten me to it and with the most marvellous news.'

She smiled adoringly at him. 'We'll open at Easter.'

Charlie had never seen her so animated in a long time. Her enthusiasm was catching. 'I can't believe it,' he cried. 'We only arrived yesterday and we already have a house fit for a king and a business to go with it.'

'What's in the bag, Charlie?'

Charlie reached into the bag at his feet and pulled out a brightly wrapped parcel and gave her it with a silly grin on his face.

25

'Oh, Charlie, you shouldn't have,' she exclaimed in delight. She tore it open and discovered a beautiful box of chocolates. She reached up and kissed him on the cheek. 'My knight in shining armour,' she said.

They broke into gales of laughter.

CHAPTER SIX

SHE'S A LITTL GEM

Pearl was happy to be back in her old room, nothing had been moved and it was exactly the same as when she had left it. The scent of lilacs filled the air and, there was a secretive look about her and, she smiled knowingly.

Ω

'I'm going to check out that car in the garage, you mentioned earlier,' said Charlie, and off he went.

Meg watched him go with a smile on her face.

Charlie threw open the double doors and stepped into the garage. The car was parked just inside the entrance. He tried a door handle to see if it would open, but it was locked so he couldn't see inside properly or lift up the bonnet as he longed to do. He had a good look at it and was pleased to see it was in good condition.

Something caught his eye tucked away at the back. He went over to see what it was. He stared in silent wonder at the magnificent two door silver Mercedes sports car in mint condition. The dust on the windows couldn't hide the blue leather upholstery inside, slightly faded with the passage of time. It was the height of luxury. The doors were locked and wouldn't open. It was the most beautiful car he had ever seen and he couldn't wait to drive it. He stared admiringly at it for a moment longer, before leaving the garage. He shut the doors firmly behind him.

Charlie burst into the room like a rocket bursting with excitement. Meg and Pearl were busily talking together and they both turned to look at him.

'You'll never guess what I've just seen in the garage.'

'I hope you don't mean, Reggie's old sports car,' exclaimed Pearl.

'You knew it was there,' he cried, in astonishment.

Meg looked from one to another in confusion.

'You can't take it out of the garage,' said Pearl.

'Why not,'

'It won't drive anywhere.'

He looked blankly at her. 'What do you mean?'

'Sit down, Charlie.'

He took the nearest seat.

'What are you two going on about?' cried Meg, looking from one to the other.

'I'm sorry to have to tell you this but, Nell sold the car engine to a fellow racing driver.'

'Charlie stared at her in horror. 'You've got to be kidding.'

'I'm afraid not,' she said, watching a young man's dream of driving it go up in smoke.

Charlie looked as if all the stuffing had been knocked out of him. 'That's the daftest, craziest, maddest thing, I ever heard,' he managed to bluster.

'It was the only way to get the money we so desperately needed for the business and, Nell couldn't bear to part with the Mercedes for sentimental reasons. So, she sold the engine. She got a very good price for it too, as I remember.'

'You can always go and sit in it, Charlie even if it doesn't go,' said Meg.

Charlie looked at her as if she was mad.

'Oh, Meg you're priceless,' cried Pearl, trying to keep a straight face.

Meg started to giggle and Pearl couldn't stop the grin from spreading over her face. They were both soon doubled up with laughter and after, Charlie had got over the shock he saw the funny side of it too.

They laughed until their sides ached.

Pearl had settled nicely in and they all got on famously

together. They worked side by side to get the place ready for the grand opening at Easter. Charlie had tidied up the front of the house and all the work on the ground floor was finished, both inside and out. The huge chandeliers shone and sparkled. The curtains had been washed and put back up and the windows cleaned. The first floor with all its empty bedrooms was still an unexplored mystery, and no one had the slightest interest in going up there. They were so busy getting all the ground floor ready with not a moment to spare for anything else.

'Well, that's me done for the day,' said Meg, smiling.

'I couldn't agree more,' said Pearl, with a satisfied look around.

'It looks fantastic,' said Charlie.

'I'll go and put the kettle on,' said Pearl, and she left the room.

'She's been amazing hasn't she, Charlie?'

'She's a little gem.'

And they both smiled.

CHAPTER SEVEN

THE RUNAWAY

Charlie and Meg were taking a stroll around the grounds before nightfall. The air was crisp and fresh.

'Look, Charlie,' exclaimed Meg, suddenly. 'There's a face at the window.'

Charlie looked up startled. 'I can't see anyone. It's probably just the evening shadows, Meg.'

She didn't look convinced.

'I tell you what I'll do,' he said, placing an arm around her shoulders. 'I'll take a look in the morning, as soon as we've had breakfast.'

And with that she had to be content.

'I can't believe we haven't been upstairs, yet, Charlie.'

'I know, but this place is huge, and once we'd started on the ground floor the most sensible thing to do was to carry on until it was finished. We'll go up there in the morning and, take a look around.'

'What was that noise?'

'I didn't hear anything.'

She looked nervously at the dark shadows in the garden expecting to see something there.

'There's no one here but us, Meg.' He frowned at her. 'I wish you'd settle down, you're a bag of nerves these days.' He kissed her softly in the moon light. 'Let's go back inside.'

They made their way back holding hands as lovers do. They slipped quietly in the side door leading to the cloakroom. They had taken off their outdoor things and, draped them over the coat hooks when they heard someone moving about upstairs. They threw each other a startled, glance, before standing very still to listen. Someone was moving about in the room above them.

'We have a burglar, Meg.'

She gave him a frightened look. 'Oh, Charlie, what shall we do?'

He put a finger to his lips and beckoned her to follow him out into the hall. They paused at the bottom of the stairs to listen. They distinctly heard muffled sounds and a door closing. They spoke in whispers.

'I'm going to find out who it is,' said Charlie, looking around for a suitable weapon. He pulled out a sturdy walking stick from the umbrella stand. 'We might have a mad man up there and I don't want you getting hurt, so stay down here and keep out of sight.'

'I'll do that.' She clung onto his arm for a moment and, whispered urgently. 'Oh, you will be careful, Charlie and don't do anything foolish.'

'I won't.' And he shrugged off her arm and bounded up the wide staircase as silent as a panther with only the dim night light to show the way. He reached the top and disappeared from view. Meg stood trembling at the foot of the stairs.

Suddenly an ear splitting scream tore through the manor house. Meg was at the top of the stairs in no time and raced along the hall. She saw Charlie wide eyed with shock staring at a terrified young woman, no more than a girl really, with the face of an angel. She cowered before him with such a look of terror on her face that, Meg never wanted to see again.

They both looked up as she raced towards them.

'What are you doing here?' She cried, taking the situation in at a glance. 'Put your walking stick down, Charlie.' Meg turned all her attention to the runaway. 'You nearly gave me a heart attack screaming like that. I thought somebody was being murdered.'

'I thought he was g-going to attack m-me.'

'You silly goose, Charlie wouldn't hurt a fly.'

The door behind her was wide open and Meg could see

into the room. All around were items of clothing. A bedside table had a silver framed photograph on it and lying beside it was a small torch.

'Let's go in here.' suggested Meg, white faced and shaking. 'I need to sit down.'

They all went into the room and, Charlie fell into the nearest chair, her screams still ringing in his ears. Meg took the seat opposite to catch her breath. The runaway sat on the edge of her bed, and waited for Meg or Charlie to speak.

Pearl suddenly appeared in the open door way. She was wearing a huge billowing white nightgown that reached to the floor, pink painted toenails peeped out from the bottom and she wore curlers in her hair. The light of battle was in her eye as she brandished a sturdy walking stick. 'What the devil is going on,' she cried, looking wildly around. She saw the culprit and glared fiercely at her. 'She's got a good pair of lungs on her, I must say. A scream like that belongs in a horror film.' She took everything in with a glance. 'My help is not needed here, so I'll leave you to it.' She quickly returned to her own bed.

For a moment no one spoke.

'I wouldn't like to get on the wrong side of her,' muttered, Charlie.'

Meg tried to smother a giggle and caught Charlie's eye and, they both burst into gales of laughter. There was just the trickle of a smile on the face of the runaway. Charlie and Meg gradually calmed down and pulled themselves together.

'Let's get this business over with,' said Charlie, looking at the trouble maker. 'Now would you mind telling me what you think you're playing at?'

There was a lost look about her.

'We aren't going to hurt you,' said Meg, reassuringly. 'Let's start with your name, shall we?'

'I'm called, Sunbeam Grey.'

'Why are you here?'

'I don't have anywhere to go.'

'Why don't you tell us all about it?' said Meg.

Sunbeam simply nodded then began to speak in a well educated voice. 'Daddy was head chef in the hotel. We had our own apartment on the top floor and we both loved it there. Mummy died a long time ago and I don't remember much about her.' She took a deep steadying breath before going on. 'Daddy died a few weeks ago in a boating accident.' She looked as if she was about to cry, but with a tremendous effort pulled herself together. 'I was told to leave on the day of the funeral. The owners needed our home for the new chef and his family.' The tears began to fall.

'Oh, please don't cry,' said Meg, and quickly passed her a crumpled handful of tissues from the box nearby.

'Fank you,' mumbled, Sunbeam sniffing and dried her tears.

'Take your time,' said Charlie, gently.

'I left with a suitcase full of clothes and with very little money as the manager refused to pay what he owed me. I rented a room in a house until my money ran out, then I became homeless and lived on the streets. It was terrible,' she admitted. 'I tried to get a job, but no one would employ me. I was terrified, cold and hungry, and wanted to kill myself and be with Daddy.'

Charlie and Meg were speechless with horror.

'Then one night I had a vivid dream that Daddy was telling me to go to an old manor house. He said I would be safe there. It was easy to find and it was exactly as Daddy had shown me in the dream. I was about to try the door when it opened all by itself. It was the strangest thing.' She paused, as though re-living the moment. 'I came in expecting to see someone but there was nobody there. It saved my life coming here,' she added, quietly.

'Meg gave Charlie a knowing look. The same thing had happened to them when they had first arrived. 'How long have you been here?' Meg asked, after a slight pause.

Sunbeam looked thoughtful. 'I'm not sure. I was ill when I first arrived and stayed in bed most of the time. I don't remember Christmas at all,' she replied, vaguely.

Meg glanced over at, Charlie as he suddenly got up and left the room. 'I won't be long,' she said, getting up to follow him out.

'Am I going to prison?'

'Don't talk rubbish,' she said, and left the room.

She found Charlie in their sitting room looking gloomily out the window. 'What do we do now, Meg?'

'I don't know,

They talked it over and came to a decision.

'Let's go and tell her.'

'It would be best coming from you,' he said.

They went back upstairs. Sunbeam was waiting for them and they could see she had been crying.

'Sunbeam,' said Meg, taking charge of the situation. 'I'm called, Meg Moffett by the way, and this is, Charlie he's my husband.'

Charlie simply smiled.

'We think the best thing to do now is for you to stay here with us and, we'll help you all we can to find a job and somewhere to live.'

'You mean you aren't going to kick me out,' cried Sunbeam in astonishment.

'Nobody is going to kick you out,' said Charlie, thinking how young and vulnerable she looked. 'Would you mind telling us how old you are?'

'I'm eighteen.'

They were both surprised at how young she looked. She wore no makeup and had a natural beauty about her.

'We have only just moved in ourselves,' said Meg. 'But of course, you already know that, don't you,' said Meg, pointedly.

Sunbeam nodded her head guiltily in agreement. She had been living a secretive existence too afraid to make her presence known.

Meg went on to explain. 'My aunt left us this house when she died. It used to be a hotel, and we're going to turn it back into a hotel. We have to earn a living, you see.' She hesitated and a moment of doubt crept in. 'We've never done anything like this before, but we have a very good friend to help us and we plan to open for Easter.'

'It's very kind of you to let me stay here with you and I'll look for a job first thing in the morning.' She suddenly smiled at them and her relief was obvious.

'What kind of a job do you want?' asked Meg, casually.

'Why, I want to be a cook, of course just like Daddy! He always said I was the best cook this side of heaven and I've won prizes for my cooking,' she said, proudly.

They were both astonished.

'We need a cook, don't we, Meg,' cried Charlie, enthusiastically.

'Oh, please, let me cook for you,' cried Sunbeam. 'I promise you won't be disappointed. I can cook anything you want. My pastry is the best you'll ever taste and my dumplings are as big as mountains.'

A look of delight spread over both their faces.

'When can you start?' cried Meg.

'I would like to start tomorrow, if you don't mind. It will give me something to do, and besides,' she added. 'It's the least I can do after all your kindness.'

'We'll see you in the morning, then,' said Meg smiling widely at her.

'No worries,' said Charlie, with a satisfied look.

And they both left the room.

It was later that same evening.

'There's some very odd things been happening here, lately,' said Charlie, thoughtfully.

'I was just thinking the same thing, Charlie.'

Ω

It was the following morning over breakfast when, Sunbeam was introduced to Pearl and told the circumstances of her arrival and that she was going to be the new cook.

'She's a bit young isn't she, but I suppose she'll have to do,' announced Pearl.

And they all smiled.

CHAPTER EIGHT

THE GARDENER

Charlie and Meg went outside to inspect the neglected gardens. They stared around in horror. The shrubbery was as wild as any jungle. In one corner stood a greenhouse old and forgotten and filled with miscellaneous junk, a wheelbarrow could be seen lying on its side among the weeds. The vegetable patch was almost invisible beneath the overgrown foliage and the grass was waist high in places.

'Oh, Charlie,' she wailed. 'This is terrible.'

'We need a gardener,' he said.

A feeling of panic began to set in.

'What's that over there?' said Charlie, suddenly distracted.

In the distance a thin column of smoke was spiralling upward.

'That's a camp fire,' he said.

They stared at it for a moment.

'Come on, Meg, let's go and see who the Boy Scout is.'

They made their way over to a small wooded area, until they saw a narrow path that snaked through dense shrubbery. They followed it and came to a small clearing and were halted in their tracks by the most amazing sight. A mysterious stranger sat by his fire, contentedly smoking his pipe. His pullover had leather patches on the sleeves and his trousers were a size too big, as if he'd lost a lot of weight. His salt and pepper hair was an unruly thatch and his complexion spoke of the outdoor life. His little terrier stood loyally by his side and growled a warning deep in his throat.

They went storming in.

'This is private property,' yelled Charlie. 'And you have no business here.'

The stranger suddenly looked up startled and his pipe fell from his hand. He stood up shakily on wobbly legs, put a hand to his brow then suddenly collapsed onto his chair. They raced up to him with looks of concern.

'I say, old chap are you alright,' cried Charlie.

'Just give me a mo,' he said, weakly. 'You bursting in like that took the wind out of my sails.'

'We're sorry for barging in on you like that,' said Meg. 'We've given you an awful fright.' She smiled gently at him and her lovely face would have melted an iceberg.

'I'm alright, lass.'

'I should never have shouted at you, like that,' admitted Charlie, red faced with embarrassment.

'You had every right.'

'It's a great hidey hole you've got here.' said Charlie, gazing about him. 'I always wanted to go camping when I was a boy, but I never had the chance.'

A look of surprise came over the older man's face.

'Would you like to tell us what's going on here?' Meg asked him with a touch of sympathy in her voice.

'Aye I suppose, I can do that, lass,' he said, with a deep sigh.

Charlie and Meg settled themselves on a fallen tree branch in friendly fashion, eager to hear what he had to say.

'My wife and son died of a fever a few months back and I knew I couldn't live in our home anymore without them so, I sold everything I had and bought this old camper van.' He thumbed over his shoulder at it neatly tucked away at the back.

Meg and Charlie glanced quickly over at it before bringing their attention back to him.

'I've travelled far and wide and been to places I'd never heard of, until I became too ill to go on. I knew that I had to find a quiet spot to rest up for a while. I came across this place quite by chance and it had a deserted feel to it and I knew it was the perfect place for me to hide away and, no one would ever know I was here.' He smiled weakly at them but his dark green eyes were pools of misery.

It was plain to see the life had been suckcd out of him with the death of his family and he had nothing left to live for. Charlie knew he would feel exactly the same if anything happened to, Meg.

The little terrier put his head on his master's knee and looked lovingly up at him with his melting chocolate brown eyes. 'This is my little dog, Scruff we've been together through thick and thin.' He fondled the little dog lovingly.

Anyone could see they belonged together.

'We have to leave now, Scruff.'

'You don't have to do that, you know,' said Charlie, as it hit him the stranger wasn't well.

'I think you should stay here,' said Meg, gently. She could see how lost and lonely he was.

The stranger was startled for a moment. 'Oh, no, I'm not accepting charity. If I stay it has to be on my terms.'

'W-what do you mean?' cried Charlie.

'As I see it,' he said, thoughtfully. 'You need a gardener and I'm your man, all my life I've grown things. I once worked in the gardens of the rich and famous. I could turn this wilderness into a garden of such breathtaking beauty,' he boasted. 'So what do you say is it a deal?'

'It's a deal!' They both cried.

They introduced themselves. 'I'm Charlie and this is my dear wife Meg.'

'I'm called Tobias Walker but you can call me Toby,' and he smiled for the first time. 'I'll make plans, just leave everything to me. The wash house needs a coat of paint, I might as well do that as well,' he added, thoughtfully. 'It's only fair seeing as I'll be using it.'

'I suppose that's it over there,' said Charlie, pointing to

it. 'Nice and handy, I must say,' and he smiled.

'We're going to run the manor house as a hotel, and we open for Easter,' said Meg, proudly. 'We've never done anything like this before, but we have two very good friends to help us.' She added, quickly. 'My Aunt left us all this in her will.' She waved her arms about. 'And we've spent nearly all our money getting the manor house ready, and we haven't any money to pay you.' She said, nervously biting her bottom lip.

'I see,' said Toby, thoughtfully. 'I don't want your money, lass. I'll be happy to do it. It'll give me something to do and that's what I need right now. I'm not short of a bob or two and can manage quite nicely on my own.'

A look of relief passed over Charlie's face. 'We're very grateful,' he said.

'You're welcome to take your meals with us,' said Meg. 'We have the most amazing cook,' she added, slyly.

'I'd like that,' he said.

'Breakfast is at eight o clock and we usually have dinner at six. We make do with a snack at lunchtime,' she informed him. 'So feel free to join us at anytime.'

'Now there's an offer I'd be a fool to turn down.'

They smiled at him then burst into laughter. Toby looked taken aback then began to chuckle and the sound seemed strange to him.

'We can have a good look around the out buildings in the morning after breakfast,' suggested Charlie, brightly. 'There should be plenty of gardening tools lying about and, I don't mind helping out if you tell me what to do.' Charlie felt quite inspired.

Toby was delighted at the offer of help. He smiled at the young man, so eager to please and felt a fondness for him and couldn't resist saying. 'Aye, I'll do that, a big strong lad like you should have no trouble digging a garden this size.'

Charlie suddenly grinned and flexed his broad physique. Meg broke into girlish laughter and, Toby was surprised to hear he was chuckling too and suddenly they were like old friends instead of strangers meeting for the first time.

They said their goodbyes and left.

CHAPTER NINE

A LITTLE SECRET

Charlie and Meg followed a different route back. The little path led them to a clearing and they were surprised to see a boating lake a little way ahead. It was peaceful and tranquil like an oasis in the desert.

'Oh, Charlie it's lovely.'

'This place just gets better and better,' he cried.

They went towards it and stared down into the murky water. It was unkempt and in need of attention, but there was no doubt about the beauty of the place.

'We'll have to do something about this,' he said, scowling as raindrops began to fall.

The heavens opened and torrential rain poured down.

'Quick, Meg let's take cover in that old boat house over there.'

They made a mad dash for it. The door opened with surprising ease and they quickly hurried in to casually stand looking out at the rain.

'We'd have been drenched in no time if we hadn't found this place,' remarked Meg.

'Hmmm,' said Charlie, curiously looking back into the boathouse.

They both wandered in.

'Oh, you're going to love this,' he said gazing at a small boat beneath its cover.

'It's a little boat,' she cried in delight. 'Oh, Charlie I can't wait to try it out.'

'There's a lot of work to do before we get in that,' he replied.

Suddenly they saw movement at the back of the

boathouse.

'There's something there,' Charlie said, suddenly wary.

'What do you think it is?'

'Some animal, I suppose,' he replied, ever watchful.

They stared into the gloomy interior and a strange face looked out at them.

'It's a little dog,' cried Meg.

'So it is,' said Charlie, smiling.

They went over to it.

'Oh, the poor little thing,' cried Meg. 'It's only a puppy.'

'How did you get here, then,' said Charlie, gently as he bent down to stroke the little black and white collie dog.

The little dog wagged his tail feebly and gave his hand a lick. It was painfully thin and shivering with cold.

Meg scooped it up in her arms. 'You're coming with me,' she said.

It had stopped raining.

'C'mon, time to go,' said Charlie, briskly. Then something on the ground caught his eye. 'Hello, what's this?' He stooped down and picked it up. 'Look what I've found,' he stared at it in sitting in the palm of his hand.

'What is it, Charlie?'

He held it out for her to see. It was a shiny gold coin.

She gave it a quick glance and a cold shiver ran down her back.

'That's strange,' he said, looking around to see if there were anymore, before tucking it away into his pocket. A sudden thought occurred to him. 'I wonder if someone has been here recently.'

'Why, would anyone come here, Charlie?'

'I don't know,' he said.

They both felt it at the same time and a strange watchfulness overcame them.

'Let's not hang about, Meg.'

They quickly left and only, Meg saw the ghostly shadow of the pirate watching them from some distance away.

The incidence was soon forgotten.

They were close to the manor house when they saw a cottage in the trees.

Ooh, a little house,' she cried.

'It must have belonged to the game keeper at one time,' he commented.

'Let's go inside,' she said. The little dog was cradled in Meg's arms, as they walked over to it.

Charlie was surprised at how easily the door flew open when he turned the handle. They both went inside and looked around. It was sturdily built. The walls were painted an off white and the windows were dirty and neglected. The floor was natural oak with odd bits of furniture scattered about the room. It had a neglected feel to it, but there was no denying the charm of the place. An idea began to form in both their minds.

'Well, what do you think, Meg will it do?'

'It's perfect.'

And they both laughed. They had solved a huge problem that had been a constant worry for them both.

'We'll come back later and sort it out,' he said. 'Let's not say anything yet.'

'It'll be our little secret,' she said.

Ω

Toby had wandered in and fitted in nicely.

They found Toby, Pearl and Sunbeam in the kitchen. They went straight in.

'What have you got there,' exclaimed Pearl.

'Oh, it's a little dog,' cried Sunbeam.

'We found it in an old run down boathouse,' explained Meg. 'And you'll never guess what else we found.'

'The crown jewels,' said Toby.

'A boating lake,' she cried, in delight.

'You found it then,' said Pearl, smiling.

The little dog began to wriggle to get out of Meg's arms, so she gently put him down. Sunbeam filled a saucer of milk and gave it to the little dog and, watched as he eagerly began to lap it up with a little pink tongue.

'Is it a stray and are we going to keep it,' asked Sunbeam, longingly.

'Not until I've made a few enquires, first to see if anyone has reported it missing,' said Charlie.

'I did hear Mr Baker in the shop say, Mr Milton's granddaughter had lost her puppy a while back and, I wouldn't be surprised if that's it,' offered Pearl.

'I'll go and see what I can find out,' said Charlie, and left the room to make a telephone call.

Charlie returned his face full of smiles. 'You were right about the little dog, Pearl it belongs to Mr Milton's little granddaughter, and they are on their way here to pick it up. He said she was heartbroken when she lost him and has no idea how he got here.'

The doorbell rang. Charlie went to answer it and returned with an elderly man of stout stature and, a young girl with pig tails in her brown hair. As soon as she saw the little dog she ran over to it. 'Oh, Scamp, Scamp,' she cried, joyfully, scooping him up into her loving embrace. The little dog wagged his tail wildly and licked all over her face, and there was no denying the little dog belonged to her.

'She's been so unhappy without him, and I'll be forever in your debt,' said Mr Milton smiling, and his eyes darted about taking everything in with interest. 'I've been here before,' he said.

And they all looked curiously at him.

'It was a long time ago, but I once offered to buy this place from, Nell after Reggie died, but she wouldn't sell it to me, stubborn as a mule she was, chased me off the premises with a pitch fork, she did,' and he gave a huge belly laugh. 'A plucky woman,' he said with a note of respect in his voice.

Pearl scowled at him. 'I remember you, now I come to think of it. You should be ashamed of yourself bullying poor, Nell like that.'

'I was a foolish young man in those days,' he admitted. 'But I've learnt many hard lessons since then.'

'Serves you right,' she cried.

'I deserved that,' he said, going very red in the face. 'I was in a similar situation after my dear wife died, and with two young children to look after, it was a struggle to keep my home together. It made me realise what, Nell must have gone through and I've always been sorry for the way I treated her. I hope when I meet my maker she will forgive me.'

'Oh, I'm sure she will,' said Pearl, sorry for her earlier outburst.

'And now I think it's time we left.' He turned to his little granddaughter busy with Scamp. 'C'mon, Patsy it's time we went home, and don't forget your manners,' he reminded her.'

'Thank you ever so much,' cried the little girl happily and wandered out of the room. 'C'mon Gramps, Scamp wants to go home now.' She called back over her shoulder.

It made them all smile.

Charlie showed them both out. He stood for a moment in the open doorway and watched them get into their car and drive off before returning to the kitchen.

'Well, that had a happy ending,' he said.

'I'll be in my room if anyone needs me,' said Sunbeam, and off she went.

It was just the opportunity, Meg and Charlie had been waiting for to catch Pearl and Toby alone. They told them about their plans for the little cottage.

'She will be much more comfortable there than where she is now,' explained Charlie.

'It's perfect for her, but you're not to say a word,' said Meg. 'It's a secret.'

They laughingly agreed.

Ω

Charlie and Meg soon had the cottage spic and span. They stood back to admire their handy work.

'Oh, Charlie, what if she doesn't like it?'

'Well, let's go and find out, shall we.'

They set off chuckling and giggling like two silly teenagers.

They headed for the kitchen. It was their regular meeting place and where they ate the superb meals, Sunbeam effortlessly cooked for them. Toby turned up promptly at mealtimes and was never late. He ate everything that was put in front of him and fitted in nicely with the others. Sunbeam had taken it on herself to fatten him up after seeing how painfully thin he was. She was like a mother hen clucking around him and, he didn't dare leave so much as a crumb on his plate much to the amusement of others and, they all adored her.

Pearl enjoyed her meals and had put on weight and looked well, gone was the worried frown and unhappy look she had worn when they first met. She had offered to mend a hole in Toby's woolly jumper and they were good friends.

Meg and Charlie enjoyed the companionship during mealtimes and loved having them all around. They had lost the vulnerable air they had both worn when they first arrived, and had a new and inspired look about them that was largely due to the help and support of their friends.

Meg and Charlie entered the kitchen like two conspirators.

'Sunbeam, there's something we'd like to show you,' cried Meg, excitedly.

Charlie had a wide grin on his face.

She looked up. 'What is it?

'Oh, do hurry up and come with us,' cried Meg.

'I have a meat pie in the oven.'

'It won't take long,' said Charlie. 'You surely don't think I'd let my dinner burn.'

Sunbeam looked at them suspiciously. They both looked very pleased with themselves. She followed them out into the garden. 'Where are you taking me?'

'You'll see,' said Meg, looking secretive.

'Sunbeam, I hope you know how much we appreciate having you here,' said Charlie, as they walked briskly along. 'And we have no intention of letting a little gem like you go,' he added, with a twinkle in his merry brown eyes.

The cottage was just a short distance away. The garden was neat and tidy. Charlie opened the gate and they all trooped up the path. The door was painted green like the garden and blended in nicely.

Charlie opened the door and they quickly stepped inside. Sunbeam looked curiously about her. The walls were painted a pale cream and pretty daisy patterned curtains were hanging at the lattice windows. Seats and chairs were nicely arranged about the room, giving it a homely feel. At the far end could be seen a tiny hall and leading off it was a bedroom a bathroom and kitchen.

'This is for you,' said Meg.

'That is if you want it,' said Charlie.

They stood quietly to one side watching her.

Sunbeam burst into tears. 'My own little home!' she cried. 'It's perfect and I love it.'

Ω

It was later that evening. Charlie and Meg were relaxing in their cosy sitting room.

'That was thoughtful of you putting that little bunch of primroses in a vase for Sunbeam,' said Meg, casually.

Charlie looked startled for a moment, then grinned. 'Is that your idea of a joke?'

'I'm not joking, Charlie.

'I didn't put them there. I thought you did.'

'No, it wasn't me, Charlie.'

'Toby must have put them there, mystery solved,' said Charlie, dismissively, and went back to reading the newspaper.

Meg looked thoughtfully at him.

CHAPTER TEN

THE VISITOR

The manor house was spic and span from top to bottom. The beds were nicely made up. The telephone had been re-instated. The fridge, freezer and kitchen cupboards were full. The newspaper advertisements had paid off and, they were fully booked from Easter to late September. The grand opening was only ten days away.

It was a time of trepidation and excitement for them all.

Ω

Sunbeam was sitting in her cosy cottage calmly flicking through a recipe book. Pearl had gone to her room to relax and read her magazine. Toby was in his camper van studying the latest gardening journal. Scruff slept contentedly at his feet. Toby and Charlie had worked wonders in the gardens and a warm friendship had blossomed between them. Blue bells, buttercups and daffodils grew everywhere and little green shoots could be seen popping their heads out of the ground. They were both proud of the work they had done. But they would need another gardener to keep it neat and tidy. Charlie was going to be very busy helping out in The Manor House hotel and wouldn't have time for anything else.

It was early evening when the doorbell rang. Meg went to answer it. She gave a quick glance in the mirror on the wall, tucking a loose strand of hair away from her face, as she passed. She opened the door. 'Uncle Theo,' she cried. She was surprised to see him there. 'Oh, how lovely to see you,' she ushered him in and gave him a warm hug as soon as he was over the step, and had dropped his suitcase to the floor.

'Hello, pet.'

She gave him a look of concern. He was very pale and had lost a lot of weight.

'I didn't realise you'd moved until you wrote and told me. By jingo, this place is massive.' He stared around in astonishment. 'I bet it has a story to tell.'

She simply smiled. 'Come and say hello to, Charlie he's in our sitting room.'

'I know its short notice, but can you put me up for a few days?'

'Oh, that would be lovely,' she cried. 'You know you're always welcome to stay with us at anytime.'

Theo had been her mother's friend since childhood and, would have married her if her father hadn't stolen her heart and promptly married her instead. She could still remember her father had jokingly called him her mother's secret lover. Theo had been a frequent visitor to their home. His jolly sense of fun and humorous stories had always made them laugh. He'd joined a local theatre in his teens as an actor then gone on to bigger things and, became quite a famous actor travelling far and wide. He'd lived in digs all his life. He had followed his dream but it was a lonely life.

Charlie glanced up as they entered the sitting room.

'Look who I've found,' announced Meg, smiling. 'Uncle Theo has come to stay.'

'Nice to see you again,' cried Charlie, getting out of his chair. 'Take your coat off and come and sit by the fire and get warm.'

'Hello Charlie, my boy,' said Theo, pleased at the warm welcome he received. He put the suitcase down and began to take off his warm coat. Charlie gave him a worried look as he took it from him and went to hang it up in the small cloak room.

'What a grand place this is,' said Theo, taking a seat by the modern gas fire throwing plenty of heat out. Although the weather was mild the evenings were still chilly.

'You both look very happy, if I may say so.'

'We are happy,' said Meg. 'And we love it here.'

'I never thought we'd ever get to live in a place like this,' admitted Charlie.

'I'm delighted for you both.'

'I'll show you around, tomorrow Uncle Theo,' said Meg. 'You'll be surprised at how big the manor house is and, Charlie can show you around outside.'

'I'll look forward to it, just as long as you don't want me tackling any gardening work,' he added, with a wicked grin. But he looked frail and exhausted. He wasn't the usual happy go lucky, Uncle Theo they were used to.

We wouldn't dream of it,' said Meg giving him a shrewd look.

'Better get your walking boots out, then,' replied Charlie. There was an air of contentment about him that had never been there before. He had always seemed so restless.

'I'll put the kettle on and make us some tea. I expect you're hungry after such a long journey.' Meg went thoughtfully into the kitchen. It didn't take long before she was back carrying, an overloaded tea tray piled high with crockery, cups and saucers, sandwiches, scones and chocolate cake. It all looked delicious.

'Here let me help you,' cried Charlie, rushing to her aid. She smiled sweetly at him as he gently took the tray from her and placed it on the table.

'A feast fit for a king,' cried Theo, smiling in delight.

C'mon, tuck in, Uncle Theo,' said Meg pulling out a chair and they all sat at the table and began to eat.

They spoke little during their meal.

'That was delicious,' said Uncle Theo, when he'd finished eating.

Charlie scoffed the last scone left on the plate with relish.

'I don't know where you put it all,' said Meg watching him. 'It's not fair, you can eat what you like and your weight always stays the same.'

Theo chuckled at them both. He could see how good they were together. He had thought at the time, Meg was too young at sixteen to rush into a hasty marriage, but he could see he had been wrong. They were made for each other and he felt a sense of relief in the knowledge. He smiled fondly at them both. 'Have you made any plans for the future?'

'Yes, we have, we're going to run the manor house as a hotel,' announced Meg, with all the confidence of a seasoned landlady.

Theo was stunned. He leaned forward in his seat. 'Tell me more.'

She told him everything. It will be known as, The Manor Hotel,' she added, grandly.

'Well, I'll be jiggered.'

The expression on his face made them both laugh.

'You'll meet Pearl, Sunbeam and Toby in the morning. They've been marvellous and we couldn't do it without their help,' admitted Meg.

'Now, tell us your news,' said Charlie.

'Well, I've been abroad for a while taking part in a film to be shown later this month. It's about a little girl and her mum and how they meet a stranger who helps them to fulfil their dreams.' He grinned at their look of surprise. 'And when I came home, my landlady wanted everyone to move out until all the repairs are finished in the house. There was a spot of damp getting through the windows and the roof was leaking in places, even the mice have left home.'

They all laughed.

'I had some time off and thought it would be nice to come and see how you were both getting on.' He made it sound very casual, but they knew there was more to it than he was telling them.

'You've lost a lot of weight,' said Meg, her face was full of concern. 'Have you been ill, Uncle Theo?'

'Just a touch of flue, but I'm over it now,' he said,

evasively and didn't meet her eye. 'I've got a bit of a headache coming on would it be alright if I went up to bed now?'

'I'll carry your case up,' said Charlie, promptly. 'Which room is he to go in, Meg?'

'Room one please.'

Charlie chuckled.

'What are you looking so amused about?'

'You sound like a landlady booking a guest in.'

'Do I really,' she said, looking pleased.

Charlie left the room laughing.

The big old fashioned clock in the hall chimed sweetly out the hour of ten.

'Come on, Uncle Theo,' said Meg, standing up.

They climbed the stairs together. Meg opened the first door they came to and they both went in. She quickly switched on the light then walked over to the far side of the room, and pulled the richly embroidered curtains across the wide window to shut out the dark night.

'By this is grand.' Theo gave an appreciative look around the room and liked all he saw. It was a spacious room with all the usual bedroom things one would expect to see, the only difference was the elegance of it all.

Meg turned to look at him with a stern look on her face. 'Uncle Theo, what's wrong with you, and I want the truth, mind.'

'There's no fooling you is there?' I was taken to hospital with pneumonia,' he finally admitted. 'And it knocked the stuffing out of me.' He didn't add that he'd nearly died, but it was there staring them both in the face.

'Why didn't you tell me?'

'I didn't get your letter saying you'd moved until I came out of hospital,' he explained, weakly.

'I'm going to look after you know,' she said. 'Breakfast is at eight, but there's no rush, just come when you're ready.' She said, good night and quietly left.

CHAPTER ELEVEN

THE MANOR HOUSE HAS A GHOST

Meg was at the top of the stairs when she saw the ghost of a pirate standing in the shadows watching her. She was mesmerised with fright. They stared at one another across time and space, and she had the strangest feeling he was trying to tell her something before he disappeared into the darkness. She came out of her trance like state and bolted down the stairs, back to the safety of their cosy sitting room where she'd find, Charlie.

He looked up startled when he saw the state she was in. 'What's the matter, Meg?' he cried, a note of panic in his voice.

'Oh, Charlie, I've just seen a g-ghost of a p-pirate.' She was trembling all over and her face was white as snow.

Charlie jumped up out of the chair and stared at her.

'Don't be ridiculous,' he cried.

'It happened just as I was leaving, Uncle Theo's room and the ghost of a pirate was standing there watching me. It freaked me out.'

'Stop talking rubbish,' he cried angrily. 'I've told you before ghosts don't exist. It was probably just a shadow on the wall.'

'And I'm telling you the manor house has a ghost.'

He was speechless.

'I can't stand it. I can't stand it,' she cried. 'You never believe a word I say.' She ran from the room in tears.

There was a look of despair on Charlie's face. Things were going from bad to worse and he didn't know how to help her anymore.

Ever since the accident had killed, Meg's parents she

had wanted to know if there was life after death. She had once asked him to go with her to a spiritualist church, but he had refused to go anywhere near such places. He was having nothing to do with so called, mediums and various psychics. He had cruelly and bluntly told her it was all a load of rubbish, and they were all cranks after her money. It had been like an arrow through his heart when he saw her crumple and the tears fall and, she had turned away from him. The subject had never been mentioned again, until this moment and he was at his wits end how to deal with it.

He went out into the night air to clear his head. He could smell the salty sea air and somewhere in the distance an owl hooted. He walked slowly around the grounds deep in thought before turning to go back inside, when he heard a strange unearthly chuckle coming from nearby. Startled he turned to look into the darkness but the night was still and nothing moved. He heard a distinct rustling in the undergrowth and saw the shape of a small animal close by. He smiled to himself and shook off a feeling of unease that he couldn't explain. He hurried back inside locking the door securely behind him before heading off to bed and the love of his life.

CHAPTER TWELVE

THERE'S TROUBLE BREWING

Charlie and Meg were arguing, furiously.

'Where have my keys gone?' cried Charlie, his eyes blazing. 'They were there a minute ago and, now they've gone.'

'I haven't seen them, Charlie. The ghost must have taken them.' She goaded him, angrily.

'It's all in your head, Meg,' and he banged his fist on the table.

It made her jump and she had never seen such anger reflected in his dark eyes before. She left the room without a backward glance.

'Bloody ghosts,' he cried angrily, before making his way out into the garden to cool off. He decided to seek, Toby out.

Toby saw him coming towards him. 'Spit it out lad.'

'It's, Meg,' he cried. 'I'm worried about her. She thinks the manor house is haunted and said she's seen the ghost of a pirate and, it's driving me mad and, I can't stand it for much longer,' he cried, looking desperately unhappy. 'I'm tired of telling her there is no such thing as a ghost.'

'Are you sure about that,'

Charlie stared at him. 'W-What, you surely don't mean to tell me you believe in ghosts too,' he cried, incredulously.

'I might and I might not.'

'What do you mean?'

'You best sit down, lad. I have a story to tell.' Toby sat on the garden seat beside him with a thoughtful expression. 'I had a strange experience soon after my dear wife, Millie and my son, Jason died. I was very ill at the time and frankly, I couldn't have cared less if I lived or died. But one night I had a strange dream and I saw them both and, they looked so well and happy and I had the feeling they were telling me to get well and, it wasn't my time and it's made me see things differently. It was so real, and unlike any dream I've had before or since. So all I'm saying, is it's best to keep an open mind, and one way or another the truth always comes out.'

'Oh, Toby,' he cried. 'All I've ever wanted was the truth.'

'Glad to hear it.'

They sat quietly together.

'Is there summat else bothering you?'

'How did you guess?'

'You've a look on your face would turn milk sour.'

It didn't raise a smile.

'I want Uncle Theo to leave us alone. He takes, Meg's side in everything and it's slowly driving us apart and, I don't know how to tell him to leave without hurting his feelings.'

Toby rubbed his chin thoughtfully. 'I see, well why not just tell him you need his room for the business and ask him to leave, and then...'

They devised a plan.

Charlie felt as if a great weight had been lifted from his shoulders. 'Oh, why didn't I think of that, thanks, Toby. I hope I'm as wise as you when I'm an old man,' he gave him a cheeky grin.

'What kind of a wise crack is that?' chortled Toby.

They laughed companionably together.

Charlie glanced down at his watch. 'It's time I was getting back. And I'll speak to Theo. I am rather fond of the old duffer, you know, even if he does get on my nerves sometimes.'

Toby watched him leave with a look of doubt on his face. 'If I'm not mistaken there's trouble brewing. She won't stand for it, you mark my words,' he said to his little dog, before turning back to his beloved gardening.

The first thing, Charlie saw when he came in the door was his car keys, lying exactly where he'd left them. He could have cried with frustration.

Ω

Meg blinded by tears collided with, Pearl almost knocking her off her feet.

'Oh, Meg whatever is the matter,' she cried, and took the poor girl in her arms and gently guided her into her sitting room. 'Come and sit down and tell me all about it.'

They sat side by side on the sofa. Her calming influence had an effect on, Meg.

'Oh, Pearl, I'm so unhappy.' she cried, sniffing and drying her tears on the handful of paper tissues, Pearl had given her. 'Charlie is horrible to me and I want my Mum.'

'Pearl spoke soothingly to her. 'When you lose someone you love it leaves a hole in your life that can never be filled, but as time goes by, the sense of loss goes away to be replaced by happy memories.'

Meg nodded her head and gave an unladylike sniff and dabbed at her eyes.

'And all marriages have their ups and downs, you know. Why, when I was first married to, Tom we couldn't agree over anything at first, but we learnt to give and take, but I never stopped loving him. Charlie's a rough diamond with a heart of gold and he idolises you and, he's a fine young man and very handsome too, if I may say so.'

'Well, he has a funny way of showing it,' and she sniffed. 'He didn't believe me when I told him I've seen the ghost of a pirate.'

'So, you've seen him, then.'

Meg stared at her. 'You knew he was here.'

'I suppose I'd better explain,' said Pearl, quietly. 'This old house has a history that goes back centuries. Nell and I would sometimes see him before he disappeared into the walls.' She couldn't help smiling. 'Nell once said that if that blasted pirate ever ruined our business. She'd kill him.'

It lightened the atmosphere.

Pearl spoke calmly, as if it was the most natural thing in the world to talk about ghosts, and not to be feared or whispered about behind closed doors.

Meg stared at her in growing resentment. 'You've known all this time and you never thought to tell me.'

'I thought it was for the best, and besides, it would have served no purpose until you had seen him for yourself.'

'I'm going to tell, Charlie you've seen him and he'll have to believe me, now,' she cried, huffily.

'I wouldn't do that, if I was you. Charlie won't believe you and you know how stubborn he is and, nothing is going to make him change his mind until he finds out the truth for himself. It'll only cause more trouble and heartache for you both, and arguing about it won't get you anywhere, so let's not say anything and wait and see what happens.'

'All right, Pearl I won't say anything.'

'You know I almost feel sorry for our poor ghost,' said Pearl. 'There's such a sad look about him, and I get the feeling he wants to tell us something and can't move on until he does.'

'What do you mean?'

'I've seen ghosts all my life,' she admitted. 'They are troubled spirits that can't move on to their rightful place in the spirit realms for whatever reason keeps them earthbound.'

Meg was astounded. 'How do you know all this?'

'It's something I was brought up with.'

'I see.'

After a short pause, Meg began to speak quietly, as she unburdened her soul to the only person who would understand. 'Ever since mum and dad died, I've wanted to know if there is a life after death. I've visited spiritualist churches, and spoken to mediums, psychics and even had my cards read by a tarot reader. But I still wasn't sure and

I've been searching ever since for some kind of proof. Then I come here and, not only do I see a ghost, but you talk about ghosts as if it's the most natural thing in the world, and I have all the proof I need.'

The relief was enormous.

'Then I'm glad for you, my dear. It will change your whole outlook on life and give it a deeper meaning than if you had never known,' said Pearl, wisely.

'Oh, Pearl I don't know what I'd do without you,' cried Meg, and she threw her arms around the other woman's neck and held on to her.

Pearl was quick to respond. It was a very emotional moment.

'You've been marvellous and I hope you never leave us.' cried Meg. 'I feel loads better for talking to you,' she added, getting up to leave.

Pearl gave a troubled look in her direction as she left the room. She knew the questions would come, and she would be ready to answer them. She wondered how, Charlie would cope with all the problems that would lie ahead, having a psychic for a wife even though she didn't realise it herself, yet.

She still remembered the first time she had seen a ghostly apparition and her stunned reaction to it. It had turned her world upside down. She had been very young at the time and, soon learned it was wise to remain silent about her psychic abilities, or she would become an outcast by those who could not see past their own nose. She could also see rainbows around people and had turned to her wise old grandmother, who the family had jokingly called a witch and said she was odd, because she could see and hear things normal people could not. She had been greatly loved. Her grandmother had told her about the rainbow that surrounded all living things was called an aura. It was the life force or energy field of all living things, including the animal kingdom and all plant life.

There had been great wisdom given to her of things not of the world they both lived in and, passed on from generation to generation.

Pearl had wisely kept things to herself and when her beloved grandmother died. She had been astonished to see her attend her own funeral. She had looked so carefree and happy and had smiled at, Pearl knowing she was the only one to see her there.

Ω

The days had passed swiftly by and all was in readiness for the grand opening. Charlie and Meg were stealing golden moments in the rose garden.

'It's strange, Uncle Theo leaving so suddenly and without saying goodbye,' said Meg.

Charlie had a guilty look about him.

'What have you done, Charlie?' She exploded in anger.

'Oh, Meg, I'm so ashamed of myself.'

'Go on,' she said, grimly.

'I asked him to leave, and said we needed his room for the business,' confessed Charlie, full of remorse.

'You rotten bugger,' she cried, angrily.

Charlie cringed. Meg rarely swore.

'It was a cruel thing to do. Oh, poor, Uncle Theo. There's no one now to care what happens to him, and I'll never know if he's dead or alive.' She burst into heartbreaking tears.

'We were going through a rough patch at the time if you remember, and I was afraid I'd lose you,' admitted Charlie, blushing crimson. 'Anyway, I've invited him to spend Christmas with us.'

'Oh, Charlie,' she cried, and smiled at him through her tears.

And all was forgiven.

CHAPTER THIRTEEN

EASTER HAS ARRIVED

It was the Easter weekend and the holiday makers had arrived in droves.

Charlie and Meg were rushed off their feet from morning till night. And much to Charlie's relief, ghosts were never mentioned.

'It's not every day we meet a Lord and lady muck,' grumbled Charlie, one day. 'They have only ordered breakfast to be served to them in their room with a morning newspaper. And you'll never guess what, Mr High and mighty wants,' he cried, indignantly. 'He thinks I'm a shoe shine boy and he said he's going to put his shoes outside his door last thing at night, and expects me to polish them, so they're ready for him in the morning.'

'At these prices!' cried Meg.

They fell about laughing.

Ω

The dining room was full.

'Pass the salt please,' asked someone, politely.

Sunbeam was busy in the kitchen. The dumplings were cooked to perfection, and ready to be served with the evening meal, when there was the most almighty racket going on in the dining room.

'You dirty sod,' cried a young woman. 'I'll knock your block off if you ever speak to me again like that.' She ran from the room.

The other guests sniggered.

'He wants his mouth washing out with soap,' cried

Pearl, angrily. She'd heard every word.

Sunbeam was fuming as she got on with the task of sorting out the sweets trolley. She had never experienced anything like the rudeness she'd had to put up with lately, and if anyone grabbed her again and pinched her bottom. She'd knock their block off.

Charlie and Meg soon realised they couldn't please everyone and, became very diplomatic. The older generation were a mixed bunch. They either enjoyed every meal they were given and, happily spent hours around the shops or enjoying a game of bingo in the arcade. They went to bed early, or grumbled and moaned at every little thing aches and pains being the main topic and nothing could please them. The Scottish guests they'd had in had been a cheerful bunch and no trouble at all. They stayed out all night and had written in the guest book, 'Beds don't know, didn't try them.'

One young couple had obviously been drinking and complained bitterly that their key wouldn't fit in the door of their room, only to find they were in the wrong hotel. They quickly left with looks of embarrassment. It set off everyone laughing who were there at the time.

Charlie had managed to catch, Mr Weasel as he was about to sneak off without paying his bill. The strange thing was the door suddenly slammed shut in his face as he was about to escape trapping him there so, Charlie could apprehend him.

'There's a vengeful ghost here,' he had cried, and all colour had drained from his face.

He had promptly paid his bill and the door had mysteriously opened for him to leave. He was gone in an instant. Charlie had dismissed the idea at once and, there wasn't a doubt in his head it had all been down to a sudden draft that had shut the door at a most timely moment.

'Where have all the nice people gone,' muttered Meg, as she dealt with a complaint. The bed leg had fallen off due to the excess weight being placed on it and, there hadn't been time at such short notice for it to be mended properly. A brick was hastily found to hold the bed leg up for one night, as the two fat ladies were leaving the following day.

Charlie had explained in his most charming manner that in the circumstances. 'It was the best they could do at so late at night. No apologies had been forthcoming from either of them.

THE NO VACANCIES SIGN' was proudly displayed in the window for all to see. Meg and Charlie were run ragged from morning till night, but the money came rolling in.

Ω

Charlie and Meg had escaped to their favourite part of the garden for a few moments peace and quiet. The scent of roses and apple blossom filled the air and colourful flowers grew all around. The birds were chattering in the trees, butterflies were fluttering merrily in the garden and, the low hum of bees could be heard.

'I'm tired Charlie,' commented Meg. 'It's driving me mad, trying to be nice all the time. It's like having a smile glued to your face that can't come off.' She muttered rudely. 'I'll be glad when they've all gone home.'

'I feel the same, but I don't know what else we can do.'

They were both miserable.

'We should go back,' said Charlie, checking the time on his wrist watch.

'C'mon, we can do this, Meg.' And he held her close and kissed her sweet lips.

'We have no choice,' she said.

They made their way back with their arms around one another.

Ω

The next set of holiday makers they had in were a joy to look after, and no trouble at all.

The time passed swiftly by. Then suddenly it was all over.

CHAPTER FOURTEEN

ARE WE ALWAYS GOING TO BE THIS HAPPY

The Manor Hotel was strangely silent and empty now everyone had left.

'I'm glad that's over,' said Meg, lying back and stretching her legs out. 'We wouldn't have survived the season without the help of our friends.'

'They've all been marvellous,' he agreed.

Pearl has been wonderful,' commented Meg

'She can handle herself, I must say,' he said, grinning.

'You mean when that awful man grabbed hold of her and tried to steal a kiss, boy did she give it to him.'

'It was a well aimed karate kick,' said Charlie.

They burst out laughing.

'And what about Toby in the apple orchard when he caught those two boys for stealing his apples and, he promised not to tell their parents if they agreed to help him collect all the apples in and take them to the store room for him. They quickly agreed and soon had them bagged up and they staggered under the weight of carrying them. We only saw them because we were in the garden,' said Charlie, chuckling.

'Serves them right for stealing,' said Meg.

'Oh, I don't know,' he said. 'I did feel a bit sorry for them, in the end, lads will be lads.'

'I felt the same,' she admitted. 'But it was wrong of them all the same.'

'We are lucky, you know, Meg to have all this.'

'I know,' she said. We could have ended up anywhere.'

It was a time for reminiscing.

'Sunbeam surprised us didn't she, when that awful creep grabbed, hold of her and wouldn't let go and, tried to steal a kiss. She had him in a head lock before he could pucker up, then she frog marched him outside the door,' said Charlie. 'It was the funniest thing I have ever seen.'

They were doubled up with laughter.

Ω

Meg found herself in Charlie's arms and he kissed her tenderly.

'Are we always going to be this happy,' she asked, smiling lovingly at him.

'As long as we are together, then the answer is, yes.'

It was some time later before they made their way into the kitchen to see the others. Sunbeam, Pearl and Toby were sitting around the big oak table enjoying cups of tea and homemade scones and, chatting animatedly away. They all looked up smiling when, Meg and Charlie entered the room like two happy lovebirds.

'I hope there's some tea left in that pot,' said Meg, smiling.

'Of course not,' said Sunbeam. 'I'm just holding an empty teapot,' and she laughed gaily at them and began to pour the tea from the teapot into two china mugs.

'Huh, very funny,' said Charlie and grinned at her. Meg gave her a cheeky grin, as they took the empty seats at the table.

'Thank you, Sunbeam,' said Charlie all smiles. 'And I'll have one of those delicious looking scones before they all get eaten,' he reached over and helped himself to a scone from the plate in the middle of the table.

Meg did the same. 'I'm not missing out on one of these,' she said, and nibbled daintily away at it, and listened to the conversation going on around her.

'It's been a bit of a roller coaster hasn't it?' said Charlie, after he'd eaten his scone.

'You can say that again, and I don't mind saying the

first few weeks were enough to turn anyone's hair grey overnight,' said Pearl, who already had salt and pepper hair.

It made them all smile.

'I had my doubts you'd be able to pull it off when I saw how young you both were,' admitted Toby. 'Just a couple of kids, I thought at the time, but you've proved me wrong and my hats off to you both, in fact, I think you've all been amazing.'

'We couldn't have done it without your help,' said Charlie, looking around. 'Pearl has more energy than all of us put together, and the way you handle trouble makers has to be seen to be believed,' he gave her a crooked grin.

She simply smiled.

He turned to, Sunbeam. 'And you're a fantastic cook. The meals you dished up were out of this world, truly amazing.'

Sunbeam blushed prettily.

Charlie turned to Toby. 'You've turned an overgrown wasteland into such a place of incredible beauty. The grounds look amazing and all the summer fruit and vegetables have saved us an absolute fortune.'

'I had a bit of help lad,' said Toby with a twinkle in his eye.

'And don't I know it,' cried Meg. 'All Charlie did was, grumble, grumble, grumble, about his aches and pains.'

'No, I did not.'

'Oh, yes, you did, Charlie.'

Charlie looked sheepish. The sound of laughter broke out as they all remembered Charlie's constant moans and groans as an apprentice gardener.

'You're outnumbered, Charlie so you might as well admit it,' said Meg, airily.

Pearl, gave him a wicked grin and a knowing look passed between them. He'd secretly asked her if she had any cream for his aching muscles.

'I don't think gardening's for you,' chortled Toby. He was fit as a fiddle and never complained of having an ache or a twinge, after working in the huge gardens. The change in him was astonishing and it was plain to see he loved the outdoor life. He had worked at his own pace and kept the gardens neat and tidy.

'All right, all right,' cried Charlie. 'I admit I did moan a bit.'

'It set them all off again, and even Charlie joined in this time.

'What say, we meet up later this evening,' suggested Charlie, after the all laughter had died down. 'Would seven' o' clock, suit everyone? We can celebrate our success, get our wages and see what we have left to carry us through the winter.'

They arranged to meet later that evening.

They all went their separate ways to spend time to doing their own thing, before getting ready for the evenings celebrations.

CHAPTER FIFTEEN

THE ROBBERY

'We've been robbed, Charlie!'

He jumped out of his chair. 'What do you mean, we've been robbed?'

Meg threw the empty bag at him. 'Here, look for yourself.'

He caught it in mid air and peered inside. 'There's nothing in it.'

Meg sat weakly down in the nearest chair feeling faint and sick, all at the same time. 'We have nothing left,' she said. 'It's all gone.'

Charlie was ashen faced as shock began to sink in. 'Every penny we had was in here.'

They looked bleakly at one another. 'What do we do now, Charlie?'

Charlie made an effort to pull himself together. 'We must call the police,' he cried angrily.

They were there within the hour. The police were very thorough but, Charlie and Meg's hopes of getting their money back were dashed, when the police informed them there had been several robberies in the area lately, but so far, no one had been arrested.

Ω

Their friends arrived promptly at seven. They were in light hearted mood. They knew something was wrong as soon as they entered the room.

'What's up, lad,' asked Toby, sharply.

'We've been robbed,' said Charlie, in despair. All the

fight had been knocked out of him.

There was a stunned silence for a moment as shock circulated around the room.

'We've nothing left,' said Meg.

They both looked devastated.

Pearl and Sunbeam were rendered speechless.

'Have you called the police?' cried Toby, angrily.

'Yes, but the chances of getting any of our money back are slim. The police said there have been a lot of robberies in the area and it's an ongoing investigation.' Charlie looked grim. 'It's my fault, we're in this mess,' he cried. 'I kept meaning to take it to the bank, but we were always so busy and I kept putting it off.'

Meg broke down in tears.

'Oh, Meg, please don't cry,' said Charlie, miserably.

Pearl went and put her arms around her in a comforting embrace. 'There, there,' she said, softly.'

It upset them all to see her like that. They wished there was something they could do to help.

'We can't stay here, now,' said Charlie, dully.

Meg stared at him as the seriousness of the situation sunk in, and the colour drained from her face. 'Oh, no, Charlie,' she cried. 'You mean we have to sell our lovely home.'

He gave a slight nod. 'I don't know what else we can do.'

'I have a few quid you can have to tide you over,' offered Toby. 'Only until you get back on your feet,' he added, hastily seeing, Charlie's look of denial. 'Aw, c'mon now, lad, don't let pride stand in your way.'

'I have some money you can have too, and you're welcome to it,' said Pearl. 'So don't get on your high horse, Charlie about accepting charity. We'll just call it a loan.'

'I have three hundred and fifty pounds, you can have,' said Sunbeam.

Charlie was stunned at their generosity. He looked around and saw the compassion in their eyes and how deeply they cared for him and, realised he felt the same way too. It was all too much. 'I-I can't take your money,' he said, with a slight tremor in his voice.

Meg was stunned too. 'No, we couldn't possibly do that,' she said, quietly.

Charlie suddenly felt weak at the knees and had to sit down, and for a moment looked completely lost.

'Oh, Charlie,' cried Meg, and went and put her arms around him and, he buried his head in her shoulder, and let it all out.

They were all very upset to see him like that, but there was nothing more they could do. There was a feeling of hopelessness in the room as they all looked wordlessly on.

Charlie soon got a grip. 'I'm okay,' he said. 'And will you please let me go, Meg. I can't breathe.' He untangled himself from her loving arms.

She stepped back and gazed mournfully at him.

'Sorry about that,' he said, red with embarrassment.

'It's enough to turn a man to drink,' cried Toby, who never touched a drop.

'This has been a terrible shock for you both,' said Pearl, quietly.

'Aye it has that,' said Toby, grimly. They meant the world to him and seeing them like that was heartbreaking.

'Can I get you both a cup of tea?' asked Sunbeam, tearfully.

'No, thank you, Sunbeam, perhaps later,' said Meg.

'We'll leave you to get some rest,' said Pearl. 'If you need anything you know where to find us.'

Toby took out his bright red handkerchief and blew his nose gustily. 'This has blown us all apart,' he said gruffly.

They were all devastated and quietly left the room.

The painting by, Gabriel Scot had also been stolen.

CHAPTER SIXTEEN

IT'S THE END OF EVERYTHING

The next morning they all sat around the kitchen table drinking endless cups of tea. They had all spent a sleepless night and it showed in all their tired, worn out faces.

'I'm going to the estate agents this morning to put the house on the market,' said Charlie, looking hollow eyed with lack of sleep. He had spent a sleepless night worrying about their future.

'It's parting of the ways, then,' said Toby, sadly. 'We'll all have to leave here, now.'

'I'll start looking for a job,' said Sunbeam, gravely. All the sparkle had gone out of her. She looked pale and withdrawn.

Meg was horrified. 'But you belong here with us,' she cried, brokenly.

Sunbeam smiled gently at her. 'You took me under your wing and looked after me, and if I had a sister, I would have liked her to be just like you.' She looked at Charlie. 'And you're like a big brother to me and I've been very happy here.' She looked shyly around. 'You're all like family to me now and I have grown to love you all dearly.'

They were all deeply moved and felt the same way about her.

'I'll start looking in the local paper for flats to rent,' said Pearl, near to tears. She had grown to love, Meg and Charlie as if they were her family and, the thought of not seeing them again was unbearable. She could see the dark, lonely days ahead. But her psychic feelings told her otherwise and this was not the end but the beginning of something new. She knew they were never wrong and it gave her a strange comfort.

'Nobody has to leave, yet,' cried Charlie. 'We can all stay together until the manor house is sold.'

'Oh, please don't leave us here all by ourselves,' cried Meg. 'It's not fair,' she sobbed.

'You will have to boot me off, because I'm not leaving until I have too and that's final,' said Toby, firmly.

'We'll stick together until the manor house has a buyer, then,' said Pearl, quietly.

'Have you thought of renting out rooms, or bedsits I think they call them?' suggested, Toby, as the thought suddenly entered his head.

'What a brilliant idea,' exclaimed Meg.

Charlie suddenly looked excited. 'I never thought of that,' he said.

'It's not going to happen,' said Pearl, flatly.

They all looked at her.

'Why, not?' cried Meg.

'Everywhere here closes down for the winter and there's nobody about and, there are no jobs to be had, so you'll not find anyone wanting to rent a room around these parts. All seaside resorts are the same,' she added, knowingly. 'It's common knowledge that landladies love to fly to the sun for the winter months.'

They all glared at her.

'W-What have I said?'

'Put your foot in it, haven't you?' muttered Toby, unkindly.

'What did you have to go and say that for,' cried Sunbeam. 'When you know poor, Meg and Charlie should have been flying off to the sun too if they hadn't been robbed of all their money.

'I d-didn't mean anything by it,' cried Pearl, looking aghast.

'Oh, please stop,' cried Meg, placing her hands over her ears to block out the harsh words.

'What's the matter with you all?' cried Charlie, looking

as upset as Meg.

'This has hit us hard and we're all upset,' admitted Toby. 'And I think we should all go off by ourselves and calm down.'

They were all ashamed of themselves and apologised for their bad behaviour, before leaving to go their separate ways.

Charlie and Meg were left alone.

'It's understandable, I suppose,' said Charlie, a moment later. 'It's a horrible time for all of us.'

Meg just looked miserably at him.

Ω

Charlie set off looking very smart in his one and only suit, gone was the casual look of jeans and tee shirt he usually wore. He was making his way out of the driveway when he distinctly heard a deep throated chuckle, startled he looked about him expecting to see someone there, but he was quite alone. He shook off the sense of unease and went on his way.

He arrived at the only estate agents in town. A sense of foreboding came over him that he couldn't explain as he went inside. It was all dealt with very quickly by a very enthusiastic manager and, Charlie was pleased when it was over.

He headed for home with a heavy heart. He turned into the wide driveway, and was hurrying to the front door when he heard the same gruff chuckle coming from nearby. He glanced over his shoulder and was just in time to see a coin suddenly come flying through the air towards him, which he quickly caught. He stared down at it in his hand with a feeling of awe. It was a shiny gold coin. He was suddenly frightened, where had it come from? He looked curiously around, but saw no one. He ran the final few yards with a feeling of panic. He opened the front door and disappeared inside, slamming the door shut behind him. He leaned against the door and found he was trembling. His heart was beating ninety to the dozen inside his chest. He did not believe in ghosts, but suddenly his world had been turned upside down. He stared down at the shiny gold coin in his hand and was stunned to think of it flying through the air straight at him, as if thrown by an unseen hand. He put it safely in his pocket and took a few deep breaths to compose himself and decided not to tell anyone of his strange encounter. He was in no fit state for light chatter and headed for his sitting room.

Meg was waiting for him as he entered the room. 'What did the estate agent say?'

'He'll be here in the morning around ten to take an inventory and tell us how much we can expect for the sale of the property. He said we would get a good price for it as property of this value rarely comes on the market, and we wouldn't have any trouble selling it and, we could expect a quick sale.' He flopped into a comfortable armchair with an air of defeat.

'Oh, well, that's all right, then,' she said, miserably.

'All our money worries will be over, Meg as soon as this place sells.'

It's something to look forward to I suppose.'

It didn't raise a smile.

Ω

It was later that same evening.

Charlie and Meg were curled up together on the sofa in their sitting room.

'I'm going to miss them, you know,' said Meg, sadly.

'And me,' he said. 'Toby has been like a father to me and, Pearl has fussed around us both like a mother hen, and Sunbeam, apart from being a marvellous cook, has been like a sister to both of us.'

'They are as dear to us as family,' said Meg, from the comfort of the armchair.

'It's strange how they all came into our lives,' said Charlie.

'They just turned up when we needed them.'

'And they needed us too,' he reminded her.

'Oh, Charlie, nothing will ever be the same again.'

'The robbery has certainly changed all our lives,' he said.

The felon had not been caught.

CHAPTER SEVENTEEN

IT WAS WORTH A QUARTER OF A MILLION POUNDS

'Think of all that money in our back pocket,' cried Charlie, excitedly. 'We can buy whatever we want.'

'Oh, Charlie, I never expected that much.'

It took a bit of sinking in.

'I think we should share it, Charlie.'

'Of course,' he said. 'I wouldn't have it any other way.'

Charlie and Meg went to find their friends. They were sitting around the kitchen table.

Charlie and Meg rushed in like two excited children.

'It's good news, then,' exclaimed Pearl, when she saw them.

'Looks that way, doesn't it,' said Toby, smiling.

'It's worth a quarter of a million pounds,' cried Meg.

Charlie stood next to her with a happy smile on his face.

'I couldn't be happier for you both,' declared Toby.

'No more scrimping and saving, then,' added Sunbeam.

They all smiled widely at them hiding the disappointment they really felt at having to leave.

'All our troubles are over now,' cried Charlie, and the lines of worry that he had worn constantly had melted away.

'And we want to share it with you all,' cried Meg, her green eyes sparkling like emeralds.

'There's no need for that,' cried Pearl, laughing. 'I couldn't take your money.'

Wouldn't dream of it,' said Toby.

'Certainly not,' said Sunbeam.

'Let's talk about it later,' suggested Charlie, suddenly embarrassed.

'I think this calls for a celebration,' cried Pearl, happily. 'I'll make us some fresh tea and let's tuck into, Sunbeam's homemade chocolate cake.'

'I've made a fresh batch of apple juice, we can have that too,' said Sunbeam. And they all looked at her in surprise. 'I've been experimenting and it's the first time I've made it,' she admitted. 'But we had so many apples and I had to make something with them. I'll go and get a few bottles,' and off she went.' She wasn't gone long.

The apple juice was delicious with a distinct flavour they all loved and, the atmosphere was one of carefree happiness as they all laughed and joked together.

The ghost appeared briefly and only, Meg saw him as he passed silently by and, quickly dismissed.

'Isn't this fun,' declared Sunbeam, giving a loud hiccup.

Toby smiled fondly at her and caught Pearl's eye at the same time and, something passed between them. 'She doesn't realise she's made apple cider and its strong stuff,' he whispered in her ear.

'I didn't know myself until now,' she replied, looking flushed. 'And by the looks of those two, they don't either,' and she looked over at Meg and Charlie.

They were chatting away together, their faces flushed with excitement and they had never looked so happy.

'They've had a lot of heartache in their young lives,' commented Pearl. 'I only hope everything goes smoothly with the sale.' Suddenly a strange feeling of foreboding came over her.

'Aye they've had it tough,' he agreed wholeheartedly. 'And I wish them all the best.'

'Those two could get through anything together. Their love for each other just shines out,' she added, quietly.

Toby was thoughtful for a moment. 'I fancy a walk, would you like to join me, Pearl, lovely name that is,' he said, shyly.

'I thought you'd never ask.'

Sunbeam had been gazing into space. 'You know what,' she said. 'I think I'll enter a competition for my apple juice. I've never tasted anything quite like it.' And she gave a hiccup.

And they all howled with laughter. Toby and Pearl slipped away.

'I feel very strange, I think I'll go and lie down,' said Meg, a moment later.

'Its strong stuff,' admitted Charlie. He soon realised that what they'd all been drinking was strong apple cider. Meg was slightly tipsy and, so was Sunbeam. 'Wait here for me, Meg. I want to see, Sunbeam gets home safely. C'mon Sunbeam,' he said, and gently took her arm and escorted her back to her cottage in the woods.

She was just about to go in when she turned to, Charlie and kissed him on the cheek. 'Thank you big brother,' she said, and slipped safely inside closing the door softly behind her.

Charlie stood for a moment with a wide smile on his face, before making his way back.

'What a gentleman, you are,' said Meg, when she saw him.

They left the room together.

CHAPTER EIGHTEEN

A CATASTROPHE OF DYNAMIC PROPORTIONS

The For Sale sign had been erected at the entrance, but no one had shown the slightest bit of interest in purchasing the property. Charlie and Meg were sitting quietly together in the garden. It was still mild for October.

'I wonder why the house still hasn't sold,' said Charlie. 'It's been weeks since the 'For Sale' sign went up and not one person has been to see it, and the agent did say it would be snapped up right away.'

Meg was thoughtful. 'I have the feeling,' she said. 'Somebody doesn't want us to leave here.'

Charlie took no notice. 'The bills are mounting up and we can't pay them all and we've had to let the house insurance go, which I'm not happy about. I've looked everywhere to find work, but it's all been a waste of time, there just isn't anything out there.'

'I've looked too,' she said. 'And it's hopeless. I don't know what we'd do without our friends help and we can't expect them to pay the insurance, as well as paying all the food bills,' she commented.

'No, of course not,' he said. 'We can't go on like this.'

They were both deeply troubled.

'I can smell smoke,' said Charlie, calmly. 'Toby is probably burning garden rubbish again.'

A loud shout roused them from their relaxed state.

FIRE! FIRE! THE HOUSE IS ON FIRE!

They shared a startled gaze before leaping up out of their seat. They raced back towards the manor house. Then stopped to stand and stare.

'The house is on fire,' cried Charlie horrified.

The manor house was a blazing inferno and flames were leaping high into the sky. Toby, Sunbeam and Pearl were all huddled together a safe distance away from the burning building. They hurried over to, Charlie and Meg with terrified looks.

'Oh, there you are,' cried Pearl. 'We wondered where you'd got to.'

'How did the fire start?' shouted Charlie, above the noise of the roaring fire.

'I don't know, lad. 'I was busy in the garden mending the trellis along the border when I saw the flames.'

'Sunbeam and I were in the kitchen when suddenly all the saucepans came to life and began rattling about making an awful racket, then the kitchen drawers flew open and everything inside was thrown out,' cried Pearl, wildly and her hair stood on end. 'We were both terrified and ran out of the house as fast as our legs would carry us. We got out by the skin of our teeth.'

'The ghost saved us,' said Sunbeam, white faced and shaking.

Charlie scowled at them both in disbelief. Meg stared wide eyed and, Toby was speechless.

A crowd had gathered and sirens could be heard in the distance as the fire brigade raced to the rescue. The heat was terrific. There was nothing anyone could do. The fire had a good hold. They all watched in despair as the fire raged. Meg saw the ghost of a pirate looking down on them from an upstairs window before the flames consumed him.'

'Watch her, Charlie,' cried Toby quickly, as Meg suddenly fainted. Charlie caught her just before she fell to the ground.

'Meg, Meg, what's happened to her,' he cried.

'She's in shock,' cried Pearl. 'We must get her to the hospital, Charlie.'

'It's all been too much for her,' cried Toby.

Sunbeam stood silently by wringing her hands, looking

wildly around and feeling useless. Pearl took charge of the situation and called to a fireman explaining the situation.

Charlie carried Meg into the waiting ambulance, and they were soon speeding along to hospital. They were closely watched by the crowd of nosy onlookers.

The Manor Hotel was burnt to the ground. It was the biggest fire on record and made the daily newspapers. It had been a catastrophe of dynamic proportions.

It was later discovered the reason for the fire was due to a gas explosion caused by a cracked pipe in the kitchen. They were lucky to get out alive.

CHAPTER NINETEEN

THEY ARE OUR FAMILY NOW

The hospital was a big grey building.

Pearl, Sunbeam and Toby wasted no time in getting there. They arrived by taxi. Their faces were creased with worry. They saw Charlie at once. He was standing in the hospital entrance waiting for their arrival. His anxious look turned to one of relief when he saw them arrive.

They hurried over to him.

'Have they found out what the problem is yet?' asked Toby, with fatherly concern.

'What did the doctor say?' said Pearl, anxiously.

'Is she going to be all right?' asked Sunbeam.

They all worshipped Meg and were desperate to hear the news.

'The doctor's with her now,' explained Charlie. 'I was told to wait outside.'

They made their way along the hospital corridor and saw the doctor about to leave Meg's room. He had a stern look about him. They hurried over to him.

'What's wrong with her?' cried Charlie.

They all crowded together.

The doctor looked around at them all huddled together then turned to, Charlie. 'Is this your family?'

'Yes, we are all family here, doctor' said Pearl, gravely. Toby and Sunbeam quickly agreed.

Charlie was too startled to speak, but quickly nodded his head.

'Well, young man,' said the doctor, addressing Charlie. 'Seeing your house go up in flames has left your wife in a state of shock, which is not surprising. We'll keep her in overnight, but she should be well enough to go home in the morning. You can go in now.' The doctor patted him kindly on the shoulder and walked briskly away.

They hurried in to see her.

Meg was sitting propped up in bed. She smiled when she saw them, but her eyes found, Charlie's first. They all crowded around the bed. The little bags of grapes, chocolates, bottle of fruit juice and a magazine, quickly purchased were laid on the bed.

Charlie kissed her gently on the cheek. 'Oh, Meg,' he cried. 'You gave me the fright of my life when you fainted.'

'You big softie,' she said, smiling up at him. 'I don't know what came over me, but I'm alright now, Charlie, really I am.'

She looked around at the others, all staring intently at her.

'How do you feel, now?' asked Pearl.

'I'm much better, thank you.' And she smiled.

Toby looked quietly on. It had shaken him up seeing her like that.

'I have never seen anyone faint before,' said Sunbeam. 'I was worried about you, Meg, but I knew you'd be alright when, Charlie picked you in his strong arms. It was so romantic,' she added, dreamily.

'I fainted once,' said Pearl. 'It was when my husband Tom, brought home a huge snake in a cage. He'd offered to look after it for a friend. Well, as soon as I saw it I fainted clean away. I've never liked them.'

Toby rolled his eyes heavenward and walked over to stand by the window.

Charlie quickly joined him. There was something he wanted to say. 'I'll find somewhere to doss down for the night, then I'd better start looking for somewhere for us to live,' he said, quietly. Charlie felt drained of all energy and the shock of it all was beginning to have an effect on him too. The responsibility of finding somewhere for them to live, almost immediately was a terrifying prospect. He looked so young and totally lost with the world on his shoulders.

'You come and bunk down with me, lad,' offered Toby, generously. 'You'll feel better after a good night's sleep.'

Charlie looked at the man he had come to respect and trust. 'I would like that,' he said, quietly. 'Thank you, Toby it's a weight of my mind.'

It was soon time to leave and no one wanted to mention what was at the back of all their minds. But the fire stood like a nightmare between them.

They said their goodbyes and left, only Charlie remained.

'I love you, Meg,' he said, smiling gently down on her.

'You look terrible Charlie.'

'I can't believe you just said that.' He grinned at her.

'I'm worried about you.'

'There's nothing wrong with me.'

'Where are you going to sleep tonight, Charlie?'

'Toby has said I can stay with him.'

'He thinks the world of us, doesn't he?'

'They all do, Meg and do you know what Pearl said to the doctor before he would let us in to see you?'

'I can't imagine.'

'She said, we're all family here, doctor and, Toby and Sunbeam said they were too.'

'Oh, Charlie, what a lovely thing to say,' she exclaimed.

'There our family now,' he said.

And they felt a warm glow go through them.

'We're homeless again, Charlie.' The tears came all too easily. 'Oh, what are we going to do,' she wailed.

'Leave it all to me and I'll find us somewhere nice to live. Oh, Meg, please don't cry. We'll get through this,' he said, earnestly. 'As long as we have each other we can get through anything.'

'Oh, please don't ever leave me, Charlie.'

'Don't be daft,' he said. 'We belong together and I will

always love you.'

She smiled at him through her tears. 'I must look an awful mess.'

'Terrible,' he agreed, grinning.

'Where's Pearl going to sleep tonight, Charlie?'

'She's going to stay with Sunbeam, it's a bit of a tight squeeze, but I think they're both glad of the company. It's a lucky thing her home was too far away for the fire to reach it. '

'Oh, well, there together then.' She was drooping with tiredness.

'I had better let you get some sleep.' He bent to kiss her sweet little face.

She was asleep as soon as he left the room.

Ω

Charlie had spent a comfortable night in the extra bed that, Toby had made up for him in the camper van. Toby had taken charge of the situation and the help he had given him would never be forgotten.

They had sat up late discussing the situation and, Toby had generously offered to loan, Charlie a small sum of money to tide him over, as he put it, not wanting to offend the young man's pride. Charlie had gratefully accepted the offer of help as he had Meg's welfare to consider. He promised to pay him back as soon as possible. Toby had also recommended a small family run guest house they could stay in, until they found somewhere more suitable to live.

CHAPTER TWENTY

HEARTBREAKING NEWS

Charlie arrived at the hospital the following morning.

'The doctor is waiting to speak with you,' said the nurse in charge. 'Come this way and I'll take you to him.'

She marched briskly along with Charlie hurrying along beside her. The doctor's nameplate was on the office door and after a gentle tap, they both went in. The doctor was seated behind his desk. He looked up as they entered. He had a kindly full moon face with rosy cheeks and a smile to melt the coldest heart.

'Ah, good morning, you must be, Mr Moffett,' he spoke with a broad Scottish accent.

'Yes, that's me,' confirmed Charlie.

'Please take a seat, Mr Moffett.

Charlie quickly sat down.

'I believe you spoke briefly to my colleague last night.'

'Yes, I did.' Charlie began to feel agitated. 'Is anything the matter?' He asked nervously.

'I'm sorry to have to tell you this, but I'm afraid your wife has lost the baby.'

It took a moment for the news to sink in and Charlie's face drained of colour. 'A b-baby,' he cried. 'I-I didn't know.'

'Quickly nurse a glass of water for Mr Moffett. The poor chap's had a nasty shock.'

A glass of water was passed to him from the decanter on the desk. He quickly gulped it down, thank you, nurse,' he said gruffly, and handed back the empty glass

The doctor looked kindly at him. 'Your wife was in the early stages of pregnancy and may not have known she was expecting a child. We'll keep her in hospital for a day or two.' There was a slight pause. 'I can see what a terrible shock this is to you and, I'm very sorry for your loss, but I think it most unwise to let your wife see you looking so upset, so I suggest you go away and come back this evening at visiting time. It will give you all the time you need to pull yourself together.'

Ω

Charlie left the hospital in a daze.

They were waiting for him in, Toby's camper van talking quietly together. They all looked up as he entered. The change in Charlie left them feeling stunned. He looked dreadful

'What's happened?' cried Pearl, in alarm.

'What ails thee?' cried Toby, his eyes widening.

'What's wrong, Charlie,' cried Sunbeam.

They all stared at him in alarm.

'We've lost the baby.' His voice was cracked with emotion. 'I-I had no idea, M-Meg was pregnant.' He stood there shaking then gave way to tears.

They were all struck dumb. It was heartbreaking news.

'The poor lad's in pieces,' said Toby, getting up. He went and put his arms around him and Charlie clung on to him like a drowning man, as he cried, heartbreaking tears.

It was the first time they had seen him like that.

Charlie felt drained of all emotion as he released himself from, Toby's fatherly embrace, once the storm was over. He looked apologetically around at their unhappy faces and pulled himself together. 'I'm sorry for breaking down like that.'

'It's a wonder you've lasted this long,' said Pearl, quietly.

'You've nothing to apologise for, lad.' said Toby.

Sunbeam looked very upset.

'How is Meg taking it,' asked Pearl, quietly.

'I don't know I haven't seen her yet. I was in a bit of a

90

state when the doctor told me. He said I looked as if I'd been hit by a bus and told me to go away and come back later.'

'They'll probably keep her in hospital for a few more days,' said Pearl, wisely.

'I don't know,' he said

'Well, let's get cracking on finding you both somewhere nice to live,' said Pearl, giving her glasses a rub, before placing them back on her nose in a business like fashion.

'And you won't need that guest house we talked about, lad. You're welcome to stay with me. It's no good being on your own at a time like this.'

'Toby's right,' said Pearl. 'You belong here with us.'

'What you need now is a plan of action,' said Toby.

It brought, Charlie to his senses. 'Yes, that's what I need, a plan of action, and thanks Toby. I'll be glad of the company.'

'I'll start looking in the newspapers and see what I can find,' suggested Toby.

'And I'll go around the estate agencies to see if they have anything suitable to rent,' said Pearl,' thoughtfully. 'We'll go together, Sunbeam.'

And Sunbeam quickly agreed.

Charlie felt inspired by their actions. They never ceased to amaze him. He had never known such a feeling of devotion as he did at that moment, not in the orphanage or the various foster homes he had lived in, or at any other time in his life and he was deeply moved.

Charlie looked a shadow of his former self, so it was decided that he stay behind and they would all report back to him with their findings.

'Take it easy now, lad,' said Toby. 'You look as if a gust of wind could blow you away.'

'There's still some tea left in the pot,' said Pearl, full of concern.

'Try and eat something to keep your strength up,' suggested, Sunbeam in her caring way.

They all trooped out leaving, Charlie standing watching them from the open doorway, as they hurried away on important business on his behalf. There was a sense of belonging and he was very lucky to have them around. He knew he could always depend on them and they would never let him down and they meant the world to him. It was a totally new and humbling experience for him and one he would never forget. He stood framed in the open doorway watching them hurry off, before going back inside, closing the door firmly behind him.

Charlie felt as if all the stuffing had been knocked out of him and went to lie down on his makeshift bed and, promptly fell asleep. He woke much later. The rest had done him good and he still had plenty of time before visiting time at the hospital. The little dog lay curled up beside him. He began to get ready as two little button brown eyes followed him about as he prepared to leave. 'You can't come, Scruff,' he said, 'I'm off to buy some new clothes.' He patted the terrier gently on the head before stepping outside. He locked the door with the little key he had been given and set off at a brisk walk, filling his lungs with the cool clear air. His thoughts full of his one true love.

Ω

Charlie arrived at the hospital at visiting time.

The doctor was just doing his rounds when he looked up and saw Charlie. 'Ah, Mr Moffett, you will be pleased to know your dear wife can go home in the morning.'

Charlie was elated. 'Oh, that's terrific news. I'll go and see her now.' He hesitated, 'Thank you for all you've done, doctor.'

'I like happy endings.' The doctor paused to watch, Charlie hurry off. 'Young love,' he murmured, with a satisfied smile.

Meg was subdued as he entered the ward, but she gave him a warm smile. She looked very pretty sitting up in bed and, he kissed her warmly on the cheek and presented her with a small box of her favourite chocolates.

She smiled sorrowfully at him. 'I'm sorry about the baby, Charlie.'

'You couldn't help what happened, but did you know?'

'No I didn't know,' she said. 'I would never keep something like that from you.'

'I'm sorry,' he said. 'Did they know if it was a...'

'No, Charlie, it wasn't anything.'

They talked quietly together and visiting time was soon over.

'I can't wait to get out of here, Charlie.'

'I'll be here to pick you up in the morning, and you're not to worry about a thing. I've got a big surprise for you.' He had a very secretive look about him. He kissed her on the cheek and left before she could ask him what the big surprise was.

CHAPTER TWENTY ONE

THE BIG SURPRISE

Charlie parked in the hospital car park as near to the entrance as possible. Meg was ready and waiting for him and smiled a welcome as soon as he entered the ward.

'What's the big surprise, Charlie?'

'You'll see,' he said, laughing. 'C'mon Meg, let's get out of here.'

They left the hospital together. They made their way over to the car and they both climbed in. Charlie started up the engine, slipped it into gear and they were off.

'Where are you taking me?' asked Meg, as they left the hospital far behind them.

'You'll know soon enough.'

'You're being very secretive.'

There was an air of excitement about him that he couldn't keep hidden. They hadn't gone far before Charlie turned off into a quiet road just off the sea front and pulled the car up at the end of a long row of neat little cottages.

'Where are we, Charlie?'

'Honeysuckle Lane,' he said, smiling. 'Come on I've got something to show you.'

They climbed out of the car.

'There's your surprise,' he said, pointing at the cottage. 'It's going to be our new home.'

'Oh, how wonderful,' she cried.

They stood for a moment staring at it. The cottage was like a picture postcard with wild roses growing around the door.

'C'mon let's go in,' he said, taking her by the hand.

He opened the garden gate, and they walked up to the

brightly painted cherry red door. Charlie produced a set of keys, inserted one in the lock and pushed it wide open and they stepped inside.

It was nicely furnished.

'It's perfect,' she cried, looking around. They went from room to room. They were both pleased with everything they found.

'I can see the sea from here, Charlie.'

He joined her by the window and put his arms around her and she turned into him, and they held each other close.

They whispered sweet nothings...'

CHAPTER TWENTY TWO

POLICE HEADQUARTERS

Charlie had lit the log fire and collected the groceries from the car that he'd bought earlier. Meg had made tea and buttered the bread. They ate their fish and chips in newspaper sitting in front of a roaring fire. Charlie was just about to tell, Meg about how the cottage had come to him, when his phone rang.

'I wonder who this can be,' he said, licking his fingers as he went to answer it. 'Hello,'

'Mr Charlie Moffett,' said a gruff voice.

'Yes, that's right,'

'This is police headquarters, my name is, Sergeant Dunn. Would you call in at the station at your earliest convenience and bring your wife along too, sir.'

'Why, what's the matter,' he cried.

'There's nothing wrong, but I am not allowed to divulge information over the phone. When can we expect you sir.'

'We'll be there in twenty minutes.'

'Very good, sir,' and he rang off. Charlie turned to Meg. 'We have to go to the police station.'

'What on earth for?'

'He wouldn't say, only that we have nothing to worry about, and you have to come too.'

She stared at him. 'Me, what do I have to go for?'

'I don't know,' he cried exasperated. 'C'mon, let's go and find out what they want.'

They were soon on their way to the police station. Charlie parked nearby and they hurried in. It was busy inside the station with police coming and going and there was a feeling of excitement in the air. They approached the reception desk and explained why they were there. They were directed to a small side room and told someone would come along to speak to them, shortly. They didn't have long to wait before two policemen entered the room thcy were sitting in and, they were formally introduced.

'I'm inspector Watts and my colleague is, Sergeant Dunn and you are, Charlie Moffett and this must be your pretty young wife, Meg Moffett, is that correct, asked the inspector, brusquely.

'Yes, that's us,' said Charlie, frowning.

'Thank you for coming in so promptly, no doubt, you will be wondering what this is all about.'

'Yes, we are.' said Charlie. Meg sat beside him eager to hear what they had to say.

The police officers took a seat opposite with the table between them.

Inspector Watts began to speak. 'We have caught the culprit responsible for robberies in the area, quite recently.' The Inspector shuffled some papers about on his desk. 'He stayed as a guest in your hotel at the end of September of this year, about the time you reported your own robbery, as I recall.' He placed a black and white photo down on the table in front of them. 'Do you know this man?'

Charlie and Meg recognised him instantly.

'He did stay a few days with us at the end of summer,' cried Charlie, angrily. 'I booked him in myself.'

'He was the robber,' cried Meg in astonishment

'Yes, and a nasty piece of work,' admitted the sergeant.

The inspector smiled broadly at them both.

'What about our money?' Meg asked, hopefully.

'All gone, I'm afraid,' he replied.

'How did you know he was a guest in our hotel?' asked Charlie, suddenly curious.

'A tip off,' he said. 'And I'm pleased to inform you that we have a painting of yours that was stolen at the time of the robbery. I'll see it is returned to you.'

They got up to leave.

'Officer Woodrow,' called out the inspector, once they were in the reception area. 'See that, Mr and Mrs Moffett's property is returned to them.'

'Yes, sir,' and off he went to come hurrying back a moment, later carrying a brown paper parcel and gave it to Charlie.

'Thank you,' said Charlie, taking it from him.

'Would you take a look to confirm it belongs to you,' said the officer in charge.

Charlie tore off the paper to reveal the original oil painting of the manor house by, Gabriel Scott. 'Yes, it's ours,' he said, with a look of relief. 'It means a lot to us.'

'Oh, thank you,' cried Meg. 'I never expected to see it again.'

They were delighted to have it returned to them.

'Do you mind if we take a look,' asked the sergeant at the desk.

Charlie held it up in front of him.

They all gathered around.

'I wouldn't mind that on my wall,' said a young constable.

'You don't know how lucky you are to get it back,' said another police officer.

'It's very valuable isn't it,' someone said.

A stroke of luck really,' said the sergeant on duty.

'What do you mean?' Meg asked him.

It was found inside the suspect's garage, to keep, I suppose.'

'Get back to work all of you,' cried the inspector, walking in on them.

They scattered like sheep.

Charlie and Meg left the station with happy faces.

The precious painting took pride of place on the sitting room wall of Gabriel Scott's cottage.

Ω

'Who would have thought we were harbouring a criminal under our roof,' said Charlie, much later.

'I never liked him,' said Meg. 'He had shifty eyes.'

'A viper in the nest,' agreed Charlie.

They sat quietly for a moment with their thoughts.

'You still haven't told me how you got us the cottage, Charlie?'

'It was a stroke of luck really. I was out walking when I met this artist chap, and we got chatting and I asked him if he knew of anywhere to rent. I told him about the manor house fire and he knew all about it as it was in all the newspapers, and you'll never guess what, Meg. He knew your, Aunty Nell then he said something rather odd.' Charlie looked thoughtful for a moment.

'Oh, Charlie do I have to beat it out of you, or not.'

'He told me she was one of life's rare gems and wasn't surprised she'd finally taken her place in heaven.'

'What a strange thing to say.'

'I thought so at the time. He told me how Nell and Pearl had helped him in the past when he'd fallen on hard times. He'd called at the manor house to ask if he could do any jobs in return for a bite to eat, but ended up giving them a fright by fainting on the doorstep.'

Meg gave a gasp as memory came flooding in. 'I don't believe it,' she cried. 'He was the tramp, Pearl told me about. Aunt Nell took care of him in exchange for doing all the odd jobs that had to be done, before they could open as a hotel.'

Charlie looked taken aback. 'That's crazy,' he said. 'And here we are living in his cottage.'

'What else did he say?'

'Only that he'd left a painting of the manor house as a gift for looking after him.'

They both glanced over at it.

'He'd copied it from an old photograph he found on his bed. Oh, and you're going to love this bit, Meg. He said the manor house was haunted and it must have been the ghost that left it there for him to find, ridiculous of course.'

He shook his head in disbelief. 'Mad as a hatter,' he said.

'If you say so,' she said, quietly.

Charlie gave her one of his looks which she ignored.

'Anyway, he said, he was flying off to America later in the day as he had a contract to fulfil and would be gone for two years, and then he said we could stay in his cottage while he was away, and when he showed me the cottage, I knew it was just perfect for us, and he only wants a peppercorn rent, as long as we look after the place for him.'

'That's very generous of him.'

The cottage was warm and cosy. Charlie had found work in a car factory, and Meg worked part time in a quaint little sweet shop which she loved. Things were going well and they were both deliriously happy.

Pearl, Sunbeam and Toby, were never far away and kept an eye on them from a distance. They were frequent visitors to the little cottage. They were always welcome in fact Charlie and Meg looked forward to their visits.

They were managing to save a little money each week. Charlie had insisted on paying, Toby a small sum of money on a regular basis, until he'd paid back the money he owed him. Toby was wise enough to know it was something that, Charlie needed to do as a matter of pride, so he accepted the payments given to him and saw Charlie grow with self worth.

CHAPTER TWENTY THREE

THIS KEEPS ON HAPPENING TO US

The Christmas festivities were under way.

Meg had bought several Christmas presents that she had hidden away, and a Christmas tree was to be delivered in two days time. Charlie loved Christmas as much as she did and they were expecting their friends to join them. Sunbeam had offered to cook the Christmas dinner and Meg had gratefully accepted. Charlie was delighted it wasn't, Meg cooking the Christmas dinner. He loved her with all his heart, but she was a rotten cook.

They were all looking forward to spending time together at Christmas.

Ω

It was the last week in November when the letter arrived.

'Hello, I wonder who this is from,' said Charlie stooping to pick up a letter the postman had just shoved through the letterbox. 'It's from America,' he said, looking at the U.S.A stamped on the front of the envelope. He tore it open.

Meg stood by watching. She suddenly felt apprehensive and a cold chill passed through her and she was filled with foreboding.

'What does it say?'

Mr & Mrs Moffett
1, Honey Suckle Lane
Sea Water Bay
United Kingdom
England
20 12 22

Charlie began to read the letter out aloud.

'Dear Mr & Mrs Moffett,

It is regretful for me to say this, but I must inform you that due to ill health. I must return home. Therefore, in the circumstances, I would be obliged if you would vacate the cottage at your earliest convenience, but no later than, December the fifteenth.

I hope all goes well with you and the financial settlement from the fire has been settled to your satisfaction. And may I take this opportunity of wishing you all the best. It would please me if you would leave a forwarding address with my solicitor, Black & Co, 33, Dobson Road.

Yours sincerely,
Gabriel Scott.

A black cloud settled over their heads.

'I never expected that,' said Charlie.

'That doesn't give us much time,' she said.

Charlie frowned and read the letter again. 'The poor chap's ill, Meg.'

'I can see that,' she said.

'I can't help feeling sorry for him.'

'This keeps on happening to us,' she cried, dry eyed and angry.

'Oh, Charlie, we haven't even a doorstep to call our own.'

CHAPTER TWENTY FOUR

IT'S OUR FOREVER HOME

Panic set in.

They had found nowhere else to live. And they only had five days left before they had to leave the little cottage they had grown to love. They were expecting their friends at any moment. They burst in full of excitement.

'We've found somewhere for you to live,' cried Toby, enthusiastically.

Charlie and Meg stared at him in surprise.

'You know the old coach house above the stables in the far corner of the manor house grounds. Well, I've been thinking,' he said. 'It wants a bit of work on it, I admit, but it could be made into a very comfortable place to live. I don't know why we didn't think of it before,' he added, thoughtfully.

The others looked expectantly on.

'So what do you say?'

'There's no way we're going to live there,' cried Charlie.

Meg looked thoughtful.

'You haven't even seen it yet,' said Pearl.

'Oh, you've just got to come and see it,' cried Sunbeam. 'We've spent sleepless nights worrying about you both.'

Charlie was at his wits end with it all and didn't know what to say. He glanced helplessly at Meg.

'What have you got to lose,' said Toby.

'You can be nicely settled in for Christmas,' said Pearl.

'And I'll cook Christmas dinner.' said Sunbeam.

It was a very persuasive argument.

'At least we can go and look at it, Charlie,' said Meg. 'We have nowhere else to go,' she reminded him.

'All right,' he said. 'We'll be there at ten in the morning, seeing as its Saturday and we're both free.'

It was a spark of hope in their desperate situation.

They said their goodbyes and, Toby, Sunbeam and Pearl, all left with big smiles on their faces.

Their mission accomplished.

Ω

Saturday dawned bright and sunny but bitterly cold and there was an icy chill in the air. Charlie and Meg set off in the old car, they still owned and was very handy for getting Charlie to work. They were both quiet as Charlie drove along the familiar coast road to their destination. They soon came to the entrance of the drive and turned in. Charlie parked the car at the far end of the drive, well away from the burnt out remains of where the manor house had once stood.

It was a heartbreaking sight.

Toby, Pearl and Sunbeam, stood grouped together waiting for them. Their anxious looks turned to broad smiles of welcome when they saw them coming towards them. They hurried to meet them.

'They're up to something,' said Charlie, quietly.

'I can see that,' she said.

'You made it then,' said Toby, with a broad smile on his face.

Charlie and Meg were warmly welcomed. They all made their way over to the old coach house set in an attractive part of the grounds, and out of sight of the burnt out ruins.

They stood in a little group in front of it. Charlie and Meg looked at it with interest.

The two story building was solidly built and the roof was in good repair, a glass window in the top would let in a lot of light, and just for a fleeting moment, Charlie

104

thought he saw someone standing there gazing down on them. His gaze travelled up a solid staircase built on the side of the building leading up to the coach house, that sat above the run down stables and, his heart sank to his boots.

'C'mon Meg,' said Charlie, taking her hand. 'We might as well go inside.'

Meg suddenly felt a wave of excitement flow through her.

'We'll wait here,' said Toby, smugly.

Charlie gave him a strange look.

'Off you go then,' said Pearl with a gleam in her eye and, Sunbeam had a secretive look about her.

Charlie and Meg went up the stone steps leading to a badly painted door which they opened and disappeared inside. They entered a room of sheer magic. They stared about them in wonder.

The living space was large and airy with white washed stone walls with a huge open fireplace at one end, logs were neatly placed there. A scattering of gaily coloured rugs covered the recently polished solid wood floor. The deep red drapes on the windows went from floor to ceiling, giving the room a sense of luxury and warmth. The furniture was oak and adequate for their needs. The kitchen and bathroom and bedroom were surprisingly a nice size, and everything was spotlessly clean. There was an air of peace and tranquillity about the place. A small bunch of wild flowers sat in a glass vase on the table.

'Oh, Charlie I love it.'

'Our friends have seen to everything,' said Charlie as he switched on the light.

'We can move in right away,' cried Meg, happily. 'And you know what, Charlie we have a home of our own, and all the land around is ours too.'

'We're safe at last,' cried Charlie. 'And we'll never have to pay rent again.'

'Oh, Charlie, it's our forever home.'

'Why are you crying?'

'I'm so happy, Charlie.'

And they both laughed joyfully and held each other. They stayed like that for a moment, before running back to their friends. One look at their happy smiling faces told them all they needed to know.

'Oh, thank you. Thank you,' cried Meg. 'It's perfect and we love it.'

'You've brought us home,' cried Charlie, and the lines of strain and worry had left his face. The years had fallen away from him and he looked just like a young teenager again. He wasn't usually demonstrative but he scooped, Pearl up in his strong arms and planted a smacking kiss on her forehead then he did the same to Sunbeam. He turned to Toby.

'Don't even think about it, lad,' he said, laughing.

And everyone joined in.

'We can never thank you enough for all you've done,' cried Charlie.

'You've all been marvellous,' agreed Meg. She threw her arms around, Pearl and gave her a hug before kissing her on the cheek. Then did the same to, Sunbeam and Sunbeam hugged her warmly back. She turned to Toby and did the same to him and his face was as red as a cherry, but he hugged her back, delighted at the outcome.

'Do you like the curtains I put up for you?' enquired Sunbeam.

'Oh yes they're perfect, thank you and I like the little vase of wild flowers, you put there too,' said Meg, laughing, gaily.

Sunbeam gave her an odd look.

'We didn't put them there,' said Pearl. 'Look around, you where are the flowers?' There isn't any.'

Meg turned to Pearl with a surprised look. 'No, there isn't any,' she said, quietly and they both shared a knowing look.

Charlie and Toby had sauntered away so had no knowledge of their conversation.

'We'll be straight back to move in,' announced Meg, happily.

They couldn't get away quick enough to start packing. They informed the landlord, wishing him a speedy recovery and left the keys beneath a plant pot at his request. And left details of where they would be living with the solicitor.

They moved in a few days before Christmas.

CHAPTER TWENTY FIVE

STAR OF THE SHOW

It was heaven in the coach house.

Pearl and Toby were regular visitors and they enjoyed each other's company. Sunbeam had started a new job as a chamber maid in a big hotel, many miles away. The hours were long and hard and, Sunbeam was very unhappy. Then one fine day the chef and two of his top cooks took ill, and there was no one to take over. The manager was at his wits end as they were always extremely busy at meal times.

Sunbeam saw her chance. The hotel manager was sitting in his office with his hand to his head and looking a picture of despair. He had been unable to get anyone to step in at such short notice and was at his wits end. He looked up as Sunbeam entered his office, after a short tap on the door. She came straight to the point. 'I'll do the cooking for you,' she said.

He was astounded. At first he thought it was some kind of cruel joke she was playing on him, until he realised she was serious. He stared at her in amazement, as she quickly rattled off her cooking skills and excellent qualifications.

'I can start right away.' She added, finishing off with a light flick of her fingers. 'As easy as pie,' she said, with all the confidence of any great London chef.

Suddenly, Sunbeam was the star of the show. Her cooking skills were put to the test and she passed with flying colours. She overheard someone say. 'She's a little wonder.' And Sunbeam glowed with pride.

The Chef returned to work to find, Sunbeam safely installed in his kitchen and he wasn't at all happy about it. He went and complained to the manager and, Sunbeam was hastily removed. Everything went downhill after that and, Sunbeam knew she would have to leave. She couldn't go back to being a chamber maid and was determined to find a job she loved doing best-cooking.

On the manager's recommendation, she was soon offered a job as cook in a small hotel nearby. She left with a smile on her face.

Ω

The weather took a turn for the worse. It was the coldest winter on record with temperatures well below freezing. Toby had caught a nasty chill and couldn't stop shivering. His camper van was bitterly cold and not fit to live in anymore. He began to make plans...'

Pearl had stayed in the summer house at Sunbeam's request. It was no longer warm and cosy, but icy cold even with the electric fire going full belt. She had a nasty cough she couldn't get rid of. The cold bit into her bones and she ached all over. She began to make plans...'

Charlie and Meg were informed of their decision to leave. It was met with a deep understanding. They had both been worried about them and could see they were both ill. They were croaking, coughing and sneezing all the time.

Toby moved into a basement flat that hardly let any light in, but it was all he could find that would allow him to keep his little dog, Scruff. Pearl moved into a poky one bedroom apartment on the tenth floor of a block of flats. It had ugly views over a noisy building site. It had been all she could find at such short notice. It was a stone's throw from where, Toby lived.

They were both unhappy in their new surroundings, but they were warm and dry. They were both too ill to spend Christmas with anyone, and stayed indoors in front of a warm fire to get well.

Sunbeam had no choice but to work at Christmas, as it was a busy time for the hotel and she was in charge of the

Christmas menu. Christmas passed swiftly in a blur of activity.

Charlie and Meg spent a quiet Christmas on their own.

Ω

A blizzard was blowing and the wind was howling. The coach house was still warm and dry and secure against the elements.

It was March, before Pearl and Toby were well enough to visit Charlie and Meg in the coach house. They had all kept in touch by phone on a daily basis and they had warned, Charlie and Meg to keep away in case they too became ill. Their shopping ordered by phone had been delivered on a regular basis directly from the supermarket. Toby had also kept in regular contact with Pearl, and a budding friendship had developed between them.

Pearl stood just inside the entrance of the block of flats where she lived waiting for, Toby to pick her up when she saw him drive up, her heart beat faster at the sight of him, and she felt like a young girl again, going on a date.

It was a short journey by car.

Charlie and Meg were delighted to see them. Charlie helped them off with their coats, hats and scarves, which they hung up on a peg at the door. The fire blazed merrily away sending heat around the room and the whole atmosphere was bright and cheery.

'Oh, I have missed you,' cried Meg. 'It's been ages since we've seen the pair of you.' They both looked pale and washed out, but she was pleased to see they were recovering nicely.

'You're looking much better than the last time we saw you,' commented Charlie. 'When we spoke on the phone you were croaking like a frog.'

'Yes, I've got my singing voice back, now,' he said, jokingly.

'We've missed you both, haven't we Toby,' said Pearl, smiling.

Toby's eyes lit up when he saw all the muffins stacked one on top of the other on a plate on the table, all waiting to be toasted on an open fire.

Pearl saw them too. 'Muffins for tea,' she cried. She had eaten very little during her illness.

Toby stared at them with a hungry look. He too had lost his appetite during his illness. 'My favourite,' he said, chuckling.

'I'd better get cracking then and not keep you waiting,' said Charlie, laughing. He went over to the table, picked up the toasting fork lying there, and expertly stuck a muffin on each prong of the toasting fork, and began to toast them over the fire.

Meg quickly set to and lathered each one with butter as Charlie passed them to her, two at a time. It didn't take long before the toasted muffins were handed around. An appreciative silence, developed as they began eating until they had all gone and, washed down with cups of hot chocolate.

'I can't remember when I've enjoyed a meal so much,' said Toby, licking his lips.

'That was delicious,' agreed Pearl, daintily wiping her sticky fingers on her napkin.

'You both need fattening up,' said Meg. 'You're like a couple of scarecrows.'

'Thin as rakes,' agreed Charlie, with a winsome smile.

'Well, we know where to come, don't we, Pearl,' said Toby, and gave her a wink.

They all laughed companionably together.

'We have a bit of news,' announced Charlie, when everyone had stopped laughing. 'We've had an offer for all the land and buildings, and we've decided to take it.'

It came as no surprise.

'What's the land going to be used for, lad, do you know?'

'The property developer intends to build several high rise apartments.'

'I thought so,' said Toby, thinking of all the beautiful

gardens being destroyed.

'We can't stay here, now,' said Charlie. He looked at, Meg. 'Go on, you tell them.'

'Meg blushed prettily. 'I'm having a baby.'

Charlie gave his boyish grin. They both looked delighted at the thought of starting a family of their own.

'Oh, that's wonderful,' cried Pearl.

'Couldn't be happier,' cried Toby.

'When is baby due?' Pearl asked her.

'It's early days yet,' said Meg dreamily.

Toby and Pearl smiled indulgently at her.

'Well,' said Toby, glancing at his watch. 'I think it's time we were getting back or Scruff will think I've deserted him.

'Why didn't you bring him?' asked Meg. 'You know we love having him here.'

'He's not been himself these days and I don't know what's wrong with him. I called the vet out and he said it was probably a chill and to keep him indoors in the warmth. That was a jolly nice tea you made for us,' he added. 'The last time I had muffins was when I went camping when I was a lot younger,' he grinned at Charlie. 'You should try it sometime and if your short of company, just ask me and I'll show you the proper way to go about it.' He chuckled loudly to himself.

Charlie surprised him by saying. 'When can we go?'

'Spring time's best,' he said, with a twinkle in his eye.

'Okay, springtime it is, and before anyone asks,' added Charlie, with a superior air. 'Women are not allowed.'

''I've no intention of going camping,' cried Meg, laughing.

'You can count me out,' cried Pearl, in mock horror. 'Not with all those creepy crawlies about.'

'Well, I suppose we can manage on our own,' said Toby, with a hint of laughter.

'You'll be lost without us,' cried Meg.

The all laughed light heartedly.

'You've perked us both up no end,' said Pearl. 'I don't

know what we'd do without you both.'

'Charlie and I feel the same way,' said Meg and she smiled. They were as close as family.

Charlie went to fetch their coats, which they quickly put on.

'Take care of yourselves, won't you, and we'll see you soon,' said Pearl, affectionately.

'C'mon Pearl, time we went home,' said Toby, and there was a sparkle about him, as he said it. 'That second hand car I bought goes like the wind,' he added, smiling contentedly.'

Pearl smiled warmly back and something passed between them that only, Meg saw.

They said their goodbyes and left.

'There's something different about those two,' said Charlie, after they had gone.

'They're in love.'

'You're having me on,'

'It's as plain as the nose on your face.'

'My love is like a red, red rose,' sang Charlie, wildly out of tune.

'Oh, stop it, Charlie,' she cried. 'You'll upset the neighbours.'

It made them both laugh.

The days passed swiftly by and spring was on the doorstep. The wild, windswept countryside was beautiful in Charlie's eyes and he loved the openness of it all.

'Why don't we go out for a walk, Meg seeing as it's our day off and, we've nothing else to do.'

'Okay,' she said. 'I'd like that.'

They wrapped up warmly.

'It's lovely living here,' said Meg.

'I'm going to miss all this,' he said.

The land was beginning to wake up, little birds could be heard twittering in the trees and spring flowers were poking their little heads out of the ground and, everywhere they looked were little green buds coming to life.

113

'I wish we could find a way to stay here.'

'I love it here as much as you do, Meg but it's just not practical. We haven't the money for the building work needed to turn the stables into downstairs living space with a staircase leading up to the extra bedrooms that we'd need, not to mention all the other jobs we'd have to do as well.'

'You've given it a lot of thought.'

'Of course, I have. I know what this place means to both of us. I wish as much as you do that we could stay here, but we can't. We must sell it all and the sooner the better. I don't want you climbing those steep steps for much longer.'

She surprised him. 'Oh, Charlie we belong here. Something will turn up, you'll see.'

'Dream on,' he said, turning his face away so she wouldn't see the look of misery on his face.

They strolled towards the cliff tops and looked out to sea. The sky was a pale blue and, the sea was gentle with soft waves flowing in and out in a never ending rhythm.

'It's so peaceful here,' she said.

'I once ran away to sea, you know, I wanted to be a sailor and sail around the world. I got as far as the harbour before I was found and sent back to the orphanage.' He gave a chuckle. 'I was seven at the time.'

She looked at him surprised. 'You never said.'

'It was a long time ago.'

They made their way quietly back to the coach house with their arms around each other.

'What's for dinner, Meg?'

'Egg and chips,' she said, laughing and ran off.

He chased after her with a wicked grin.

CHAPTER TWENTY SIX

A LETTER ARRIVES

It was the middle of the week when the letter arrived. It was from a firm of solicitors unknown to them. Charlie opened it and began to read it. Meg waited expectantly to hear what he had to say.

'Gabriel has passed away,' he said, sadly.

There was a slight pause. 'When did he die, Charlie?'

'Three weeks ago and the funeral was last week.'

'He must have known he was very ill and that's why he wanted us out of the cottage, so quickly, so he could die at home. I hope he got his wish.'

'Yes, he did, it says that he died peacefully in his sleep at home.' Charlie read on and his mouth fell open. 'He's left us his cottage, Meg.'

'He's what!'

They were both stunned.

'The solicitor requests our presence at the reading of the will on Monday morning at ten o clock in their office in Keyhole Court,' said Charlie, as he finished reading the letter.

They left the solicitors office in a daze.

Honeysuckle cottage was officially theirs. Gabriel had left his money to various charities named in the will. He had been a well known artist and a very rich man.

They set off to Honeysuckle cottage.

Meg turned the key in the lock and pushed the door open and they both stepped inside. It was just as they remembered it and, they fell in love with it all over again. The walls had been stripped bare of all drawings and paintings and anything personal had been removed. Only the big furniture remained for their use. The cottage had an empty feel to it.

They stood gazing about them.

'Oh, Charlie I love it.'

'A dream home,' said Charlie and felt a great sense of relief.

They left their new home with a feeling of joy and all their troubles had melted away.

'I bet Toby and Pearl will be bowled over when we tell them,' said Charlie.

Toby and Pearl were astonished at their good news. They were congratulated warmly and said it was well deserved. Pearl remembered Gabriel, and said he'd been a fine young man and a superb artist.

They received another letter the following day. It was from a firm of solicitors, informing them the exchange of contract for the sale of the manor house land, including all outbuildings was ready to be signed, and with due respect, would they please call in at their earliest convenience to complete the sale.

'Everything's happening at once,' said Meg.

'I wish we could keep it all,' he said. 'Oh, don't get me wrong, I'm looking forward to making the cottage our home. I love it as much as you do.'

They stood in a muddle of cardboard boxes full of their things.

'We can't stay here, Charlie. We have our future to think of now.'

'I'll ring up in the morning and make the appointment.'

'It's for the best, Charlie.

'I know,' he agreed. 'I only wish I didn't love it so much here as well.'

'Go for a walk, Charlie and let me get on with the packing. You're hopeless do you know that and, I'm better off without you under my feet all the time.' Her emotions were all over the place and she snapped at him.

'You've been a moody cow lately,' he snapped back.

'Oh, I'm sorry Charlie,' and she began to cry. 'I don't know what's wrong with me these days.'

He went and put his arms around her and held her close.

Then the most amazing thing happened and they both stood absolutely still.

'Did you feel that,' she said, wonderingly.

'Is that what I think it is?'

It happened again.

'It's our baby kicking me, Charlie.'

They were both spellbound.

'Incredible isn't it,' said Charlie, when nothing else happened and, he released her with a look of awe.

They settled down after a while, but everything had changed between them when they realized it had been Meg's hormones giving her the moody blues. Charlie couldn't stop smiling. He was going to be a dad.

'Why don't you go out for a walk, Charlie and I'll go for a lie down.'

'Are you sure,' he asked, hesitantly.

'Yes, I want you to.'

'All right, but I won't be long.' He went to collect his outdoor things and soon left.

Meg sat quietly by the fireside deep in thought when unexpectedly, she had a fleeting vision of greenery and a beautiful landscape and a feeling of incredible happiness swept over her.

'Peace and happiness lies ahead,' said the voice in her head, and she knew it was her Aunty Nell speaking to her.

'If you say so,' she said, drowsily.

Meg soon dozed off.

CHAPTER TWENTY SEVEN

GHOSTS OF THE PAST

It was late in the day when, Charlie strolled leisurely along through the spacious gardens and windswept countryside. He took the familiar path that led to the high cliffs, overlooking a wild and windswept sea. The beauty of it all took his breath away and he loved the wildness of it all, and wished he didn't have to sell all he held dear. He stood there taking it all in when suddenly, the ground beneath his feet caved in and he was falling, falling down, down into darkness to land with a thud as he reached the hard rocky floor. He slowly got to his feet feeling slightly dazed, but with no serious injury. He was in a huge cavern looking out to sea. He could hear the sea pounding against the rocks just beneath where he stood. The evening shadows flooded in from outside giving everything an eerie atmosphere.

He was looking out to sea and to his amazement saw a pirate ship with the skull and cross bones flying from the mast. He stood transfixed with wonder as the ghosts of the past sailed gently away into the distance. He stared out to sea long after it had gone and only a silvery moon remained in the dark night sky.

Charlie knew without a shadow of doubt he had seen a ghost pirate ship. He finally turned his back on the sea to look into the dark cave. He switched on a little torch that he always carried in his pocket, and shone a thin beam of light around.

His astonished gaze took in dozens of round barrels with wooden taps fitted in the bottom half of each one. They were piled one on top of the other in neat rows all

118

along the back wall of the cave. He guessed they would be full of rum, a sailor's favourite tipple. His eyes fell on all the caskets and, sea chests scattered about with open lids that couldn't close because they overflowed with sparkling diamonds, glittering emeralds, awesome rubies, pearl necklaces and gold coins. He stared in wonder and disbelief, as he made his way over to them to stand looking down on the most magnificent jewels he had ever seen. He stooped down to pick up a handful of rubies and other precious stones, gold coins trickled through his fingers.

He was as excited as a school boy. He had found the pirate treasure that had lain hidden for centuries. He began to fill his coat pockets with as many precious jewels he could carry, before looking for a way out. He saw a stone staircase to one side leading up. He made his way over to it and began to climb. He made steady progress until he came to a trap door in the roof. He pushed it open and it split in half with a groan of broken timber, worn and rotted with age. He finally climbed out to find he was in a densely populated part of the grounds, surrounded by thick, overgrown shrubbery all around. It was too dark for him to get his bearings.

He shone the torch around and was amazed to see he was behind some shrubbery where Toby's camper van had been. He followed a little winding path that he knew would take him home. It was an eerie feeling to be walking along the same route smugglers and pirates had once trod.

He burst into the room like an express train. Meg looked up startled. She was astonished to see, Charlie's dirty hands and grubby face and his clothes were a mess. His eyes were shining like stars.

'Oh, Meg, come and see what I've found.'

He went over to the table, and placing his hands in his pockets, carefully took out the precious gems and began to place them gently on the table in front of him. The table was soon covered with a glittering display of diamonds, rubies, gold sovereigns, emeralds, rings and jade necklaces. They sparkled and shone in the soft lighting in the room.

Meg reverently touched one or two before turning to Charlie in astonishment. 'Where did you find them?'

'Deep underground,' he said, taking off his coat and draped it over the nearest chair.

'It's a king's ransom,' she said, all starry eyed.

'I was walking along the cliff tops when suddenly the ground gave way beneath me and I fell into this huge cave that looked out to sea.'

'Oh, Charlie, you were lucky you weren't hurt.'

'I was looking out to sea when I saw the pirate ghost ship, Meg and I saw the skull and cross bones flying from the mast.'

'Oh, how marvellous, I wish I'd seen it. Oh, now I understand!' She exclaimed. 'The pirate has been haunting the manor house for hundreds of years, and he couldn't rest until someone found his treasure.'

'Do you think he's gone, now?'

'I'm sure of it,' she said.

'We'll have to tell someone, Charlie.'

'Let's keep it to ourselves for the time being.'

'Oh, Charlie, we're rich as kings.'

'And Queens,' he said, laughing.

They threw their arms around one another and danced wildly around the room until they were both breathless.

CHAPTER TWENTY EIGHT

A WORLDWIDE SENSATION

The following morning they promptly cancelled the sale. They told Toby and Pearl something of great importance had taken place and would they please come and see them as soon as possible.

They quickly hurried round.

'It's like looking at the crown jewels,' gasped Toby.

Pearl, for once, was speechless as she stared at the glittering array of precious jewels, sparkling and winking up at her in the cold light of day.

Meg had also said the same thing to Sunbeam over the telephone. She had arrived within the hour after leaving explicit instructions to the temporary cook in her absence.

Sunbeam stared in amazement at all the precious gems spread out in front of her on the table. It was a breathtaking sight, and one they would never forget.

The authorities were informed of their amazing find. Things moved fast after that. The treasure was removed expertly and efficiently from its secret hiding place in the huge cave and taken to a place of safety and sold to the highest bidder. Several of the rarest gems were donated to the British Museum for public display. It was gratefully received.

It was a worldwide sensation that captured the imagination and was in all the newspapers. And it came to light that the manor house had a past history, it was well documented and some reports claimed it was haunted.

John Black of dubious reputation had bought the manor house and lived there his entire life. It was discovered on his death that he had been a pirate sailing the high seas, although he was never caught. The truth was only discovered when he was later found in the grounds of his home, still dressed as a pirate and suffering appalling injuries from gunshot wounds from which he never recovered. His sailing ship, Sea Horse was also later found abandoned on the rocks and slowly sank to the bottom of the ocean. Rumour has it that on a wild and stormy night the ghost ship, Sea Horse can still be seen with its sails billowing gently as it drifts silently away into the darkness.

Ω

Charlie and Meg were stunned when they received a huge cheque for over eight million pounds. They had wanted to share the money equally but, Toby, Pearl and Sunbeam had all refused, saying it was too much. They agreed to accept one million pounds each.

The search began to buy a new home.

CHAPTER TWENTY NINE

A BRILLIANT IDEA

The sun shone weakly from a clear blue sky, as Charlie and Meg moved their things out of the coach house and into Honeysuckle cottage. They had kept their address secret from reporters and nosy onlookers who had invaded their peace and quiet, bombarding them with questions. They were overjoyed with their new home and soon settled in. They were expecting their friends around at any moment.

There was a knock on the door.

'Hello is anyone home,' called a familiar voice.

'Come in, Pearl,' called Meg, from inside.

Sunbeam and Toby followed her in with, Scruff between them, wagging his tail so fast, it's a wonder it didn't drop off.

They sat companionably around asking after everyone's health.

'By it's a grand afternoon,' said Toby, conversationally. 'The gardens are beginning to look alive again.' They all knew how much he missed his beloved gardening The little vase of wild flowers on the window sill caught his eye. 'They're pretty,' he said.

Charlie turned to Meg. 'I think now is a good time to tell them, don't you?'

'Yes, I do,' she said.

They had everyone's attention.

'We thought we'd turn the Manor House grounds into a public park,' said Charlie.

A wave of excitement went around the room. And before anyone could get a word in, Charlie began telling them all about their plans for the future.

'There isn't a public park for miles around and we think this would be the ideal spot, and we'd like to turn the summer house into a cafe with a seating area outside. And we could add an adventure playground where your old camper van was, Toby before you had it towed away,' he added enthusiastically.

'And we could use the cave, as well,' broke in Meg, excitedly.

Charlie saw at once what she meant. 'That's clever thinking, Meg.'

'We could put in some fake jewellery and lots of other bits and bobs to make it look real,' she said, and suddenly gave a wicked grin. 'We'll need an actor to play the part of a pirate and tell exciting stories to children, and we could have pirate workshops and a dressing up stage in the old stables. The coach house is there for us all to use whenever we want, and I'm sure it'll come in handy for something.'

'What a brilliant idea,' exclaimed Pearl, getting caught up in the excitement of it all.

'Fantastic,' agreed Toby. 'And who is going to play the part of a pirate?'

'I might know someone who fits the bill,' said Meg, and burst out laughing.

'I can't wait to see his face, when we tell him,' chortled Charlie.

'Oh, poor, Uncle Theo,' she cried, doubled up with mirth.

They all started to laugh.

Charlie resumed telling them the rest of the plan as soon as they had all quietened down. 'We want you to be park superintendant, Toby, so what do you say?'

'I'm the man for the job.' And he beamed at him.

'Sunbeam, we'd like you to run the cafe,' cried Meg.

'Oh, how marvellous, I'd love that.'

'You bake such smashing pies and your chocolate cake is out of this world, said Charlie, and,' he added, on a more serious note. 'You will be here with us where you belong with people who care about you.'

And they all agreed.

'You seem to have thought of everything,' said Toby.

Pearl looked around at their happy smiling faces and felt left out, as she realised there was nothing she could do that would be of any use.'

Meg turned to Pearl, as if she'd read her thoughts. 'Charlie and I would love you to be Godmother to our baby.' She smiled when she saw the look of delight on Pearl's face.

'Oh, really,' she cried. 'I would love to that, and I've nearly finished knitting a matinee coat for the baby.' She was all rosy with enthusiasm.

'It's my turn to give everyone tea next, Sunday' said Sunbeam, eagerly.

'And it's my turn the week after,' cried Pearl, smugly and they both laughed. 'And what about you, Toby,' enquired Pearl, cheekily.

'Like I said before, you're all welcome anytime, as long as you don't expect me to get the rolling pin out and start baking,' he replied, laughing.

They prepared to leave. They had all bought a small home by the sea all within walking distance of one another. They were all very happy.

They said a cheerful goodbye and left.

Ω

The building work went ahead without a hitch and was soon finished. A beautiful rose garden was in place where the manor house had once stood with an attractive gazebo situated close by. The gardener's cottage that had been, Sunbeam's little home was now a cafe with a picnic area outside.

The boating lake had been restored to its original charm, along with several little rowing boats for hire at a reasonable cost.

A play area complete with swings and slide and other

climbing equipment was in another area with plenty of seats around for mums and dads to sit on. The huge cave was filled with pirate treasure, A make believe pirate ship was the entrance, leading down to the cave, and safety rails had been fitted to the sides of a staircase. Colourful lights had been added to light up the inside making it look spectacular eerie. The stables had been transformed inside into a stage for plays and, pirate outfits had been added.

Toby had worked hard in the gardens, making it as attractive as possible with a marvellous display of flowers. The hedges were neatly trimmed and cut back to make way for new pathways through the park. It had been well advertised and a big write up had been in the local newspaper advertising the grand opening of, Manor Park, on the first Saturday in June in three weeks time.

There was only one thing missing. They were all anxiously waiting for Theo to arrive.

Ω

Theo had been surprised to receive a letter from, Meg telling him to drop everything and come and see them without delay, as they had some exciting news they wanted to share with him. It was brief and to the point.

He'd promptly packed an overnight bag and took the first train that would take him there. After a long journey he finally arrived at his destination. There was no one at the station to meet him, as he hadn't been sure of the time he would be arriving. He jumped in a taxi for the short journey to Meg and Charlie's cottage. He arrived on the doorstep at teatime and knocked on the brightly painted red door.

It was quickly opened. 'You made it then,' cried Meg, ushering him in.

'Nice to see you again,' said Charlie, warmly. 'Come on through.'

'I'm delighted to be here,' said Theo. 'And I'm bursting with curiosity to see why you have summoned me

126

here at such short notice.'

There was no ill feeling about his hasty departure the last time they met. They went into the living room, everyone was there waiting to greet him. Theo looked around at them all smiling back at him with a knowing look. There was a feeling of expectancy in the air.

'Why don't you come and sit down and take your coat off and I'll tell you everything,' said Charlie, eagerly.

As soon as he was seated and a cup of tea in his hand, Charlie explained to, Theo about their plans for Manor Park.

'And what we need now is someone who can act the part of a pirate. So will you do it?'

There was absolute silence.

'Me!' he cried, in astonishment. 'You want me to come here and dress up as a pirate.'

'We couldn't do it without you,' said Charlie, with a cheeky grin and his eyes sparkled with merriment.

'By Jingo, I'll do it.'

The place was in uproar, as they all shouted, hip, hip, hooray, and sang for he's a jolly good fellow. It was sometime before things returned to normal and they were quietly talking together.

The teapot was re-filled and sandwiches were passed around.

'I have some news I want to share with you,' said Pearl. 'Toby has asked me to marry him.' She was blushing furiously. 'And I said yes.'

Toby looked proudly on.

'Oh, very good,' cried Meg. 'I'm very happy for you.'

'Congratulations,' said Sunbeam. 'I'll make your wedding cake.'

Charlie congratulated them both warmly. And Theo gave them his warmest regards.

'Toby will be selling his bungalow if anyone is interested.' She looked directly at, Theo looking relaxed and happy.

'I'll have it,' he said, and could well afford it thanks to,

Meg and Charlie's generosity.

'Have you set a date for the wedding, yet,' asked Meg.

'As a matter of fact we have,' said Pearl. 'We're having a quiet wedding in the registry office next, Saturday at two' o' clock and everyone is welcome.'

And they all smiled at her.

CHAPTER THIRTY

A GRAND DO

The wedding was a quiet affair.

Pearl was dressed in a cream outfit with matching accessories and carried a small posy of flowers. Toby was well turned out in a dark suit with his hair trimmed and combed into order. Their happiness was plain to see.

They all attended the wedding beautifully dressed. Meg's outfit was blue like the sky on a summer's day. Sunbeam wore a pretty daisy patterned dress. Charlie looked very handsome in his new suit and so did, Theo.

It was a very happy occasion. The vows were said and they left the registry office with everyone following on behind. Snap shots were taken and Pearl threw her bouquet of small flowers over her shoulder, they were caught by an astonished, Sunbeam. The reception was held in the Bay Hotel in a posh part of town. The food was delicious and the champagne flowed freely. Charlie gave a speech about some of, Toby's antics in the garden that made them laugh. The champagne went straight to Pearl's head and she constantly giggled. Sunbeam was flushed and starry eyed at all the champagne she drank and hiccupped loudly. Theo sat at a table smiling around at everyone with a glazed expression on his face, occasionally sipping champagne from his glass

It was a hilarious event.

Meg soon to be a mother had refused all alcohol and had wisely drunk only fruit juice. Then all too soon it was over as the happy couple prepared to leave for their two weeks in the sun.

'I expect that Scruff will want his walk when we get

back,' said Meg, smiling as they waved off the happy couple.

The little dog had become part of the family now and, always made himself quite at home when he was with them.

'It was a grand do,' remarked, Theo standing beside them.

CHAPTER THIRTY ONE

A NEW LIFE

Meg suddenly bent double with pain. The baby's coming. The baby's coming,' she yelled.

Charlie jumped to his feet. 'What now!'

'Yes, you idiot, now, get me to the hospital, Charlie. Ooh, it hurts.'

Charlie grabbed Meg's hospital bag tucked neatly away in the corner of the room, snatched his car keys off the table. They rushed off to the hospital. Charlie drove like the wind. They reached the hospital in record time. Meg was quickly whisked away to the delivery room.

It wasn't long before the baby was born. Charlie was the proud father of a baby son. He telephoned Pearl, Toby and Sunbeam to tell them the good news.

They couldn't wait to get there.

Ω

They arrived within the hour.

They were all flushed with happiness.

'Oh, isn't he beautiful,' cried Sunbeam, unable to take her eyes of the cute little baby.

'He's adorable,' said Pearl, gazing at him lovingly.

'He's a little smasher,' said Toby, turning to shake, Charlie by the hand. 'Congratulations lad.'

Charlie just grinned.

'We've decided to call him Gabriel,' said Meg.

They all smiled in understanding and said it was a lovely name. Visiting time was almost over and it was time to leave.

They left the room without disturbing the child fast asleep in his cot. Charlie remained for a few moments longer. He couldn't tear his eyes away from their sleeping child.

'We're a family now, Charlie.'

'And what could be more wonderful than that,' he said.

Ω

They left the hospital the following morning with their baby son snuggled up in warm clothes. Their friends popped in later in the day to see them. They brought presents for the new baby fast asleep in his cradle, made by Toby out of oak that would last a lifetime. Pearl brought a couple of matinee jackets she had knit and, Sunbeam had bought a romper suit and a toy rattle. They admired the little treasure sleeping soundly in his cradle, while the doting parents looked on.

It was a happy time.

'I have something to say,' said Meg to everyone in the room. 'Who else knew about the ghost?'

There was a moment of stunned silence.

'I first saw the ghost after I'd moved in with Nell,' confessed Pearl. 'She told me he'd been haunting the manor house for centuries and, must have been a pirate in his lifetime. She was very calm and matter of fact about it, and it wasn't the first time I'd seen a ghost, although, I must admit, I did wonder what kept him from moving on.'

They all stared at her in amazement.

'I've seen him a few times, too,' admitted Toby. And they all turned to look at him. 'It was always late at night when I saw him walking along the cliff tops on his way to the sea. He was in full pirate dress with cutlass, and everything a pirate would need to plunder the high seas. He was a magnificent and terrifying sight. It gave me the shivers, I can tell you,' he added, sheepishly.

'I've seen him, too,' said Sunbeam.

'You kept that quiet,' cried Meg, in astonishment.

Charlie sat dumbfounded by it all.

'I used to hear his footsteps walking past my room late at night. I would lock my door and put my head under the bedclothes, shaking like a leaf. Then one morning I saw a red rose on the floor outside my door and I knew he'd left it there for me. Then one night it was very late, but I couldn't sleep so I went down to the kitchen to make myself a cup of hot chocolate, and was on my way back to my room when I saw him. He smiled at me and gave a sweeping bow I was never frightened after that.' She sighed dreamily. 'He was so handsome.'

They all stared at her in astonishment.

'I've seen him too,' admitted Theo.

They all turned to look at him.

'He was walking through the grounds. I thought it was the evening shadows at first, but there was no mistake. It was the ghost of a pirate and he was heading for the cliff tops. He was gone in seconds, but I knew right away he was the ghost that haunted the manor house.'

'I saw him on the first day we arrived at the manor house,' said Meg.

Charlie looked ashamed.

'I was alone at the time as, Charlie had wandered off into another room. I was looking at an old photograph and when I turned around I saw the ghost of a pirate watching me then he disappeared. I did tell you at the time, Charlie but you didn't believe me and thought I was making the whole thing up.'

'I'm sorry, Meg,' he said, full of remorse.

'Apology accepted,' was all she said.

'Something strange happened to me, too,' admitted Charlie

Meg looked surprised. 'Don't tell me you've seen him too.'

'Not exactly,' he said, quietly.

'This should be interesting,' said Toby.

They were all agog to hear what he had to say.

'It was the day I was going to the estate agents, when I

thought I heard a man's gruff voice call out, but when I looked around there was no one there, so I put it down to the wind in the trees, or some such thing,' and he shrugged. 'But it was on my way back when I heard a man's deep laugh. But when I looked around there was no one there. Then a gold coin flew through the air heading straight for me, just as if someone had thrown it. I caught it in my hand, and I've never been so scared in all my life.'

They were all flabbergasted.

'All this time he's been trying to tell someone about the treasure, and he chose you, Charlie,' said Meg, thoughtfully, and they all agreed with her.

'Nothing will surprise me, after this,' he said.

They were all stunned into silence.

'He will have gone to his eternal resting place, now,' said Pearl softly. 'And may he rest in peace.'

'Amen, to that,' murmured, Meg.

'Amen,' they all said.

'We've all been shown that life is eternal,' said Pearl, wisely. 'And love never dies.' The strong scent of lilacs filled the room. 'Nell is here,' she added, quietly. 'It was Nell that opened the door to welcome you in when you first arrived,' she explained.

'I thought so,' said Meg, and Sunbeam quickly agreed with her.

The corner of the room was suddenly cloaked in a brilliant white light, and a figure began to appear. 'Daddy,' whispered, Sunbeam in awe. 'I can see daddy and he's smiling at me.'

They all looked on in stunned silence as he gently faded away to be replaced by a man and a woman.

'It's my mum and dad,' cried Meg, as two smiling faces looked back at her, before they too gently faded away.

Then they heard a child cry out. 'Daddy we love you.' On Toby's face was a look of amazement that quickly changed to joy, and a red rose appeared on his lap.

An even brighter light began to fill the room and a man

in a navel uniform stood beside a lovely young woman. 'You are our dearly beloved son, Charlie,' said the sea captain. 'I drowned at sea when you were a few weeks old.'

'I'm your mother,' said the beautiful lady. 'I was dying and I had to leave you where you would be well looked after. We want you know you were dearly loved and, not just an unwanted child given away. We will always love you, Charlie,' said his mother.' They both faded away.

Charlie was speechless with joy and his eyes filled with tears of happiness.

Tears shone in everyone's eyes and before anyone could say anything.

The ghost of a pirate stood there, before changing into lord of the manor, and they all recognised him from the painting. 'I can leave you now,' was all he said. He was gone in an instant.

They were all deeply moved at what had taken place.

CHAPTER THIRTY TWO

MANOR PARK

Manor Park was a roaring success. The shrubbery was neatly trimmed and everywhere flowers flourished in gay abandon bringing a riot of colour that was amazing to see. The lawns were well attended and the winding pathways were magical to walk through. The cafe was a huge success. Sunbeam never tired of thinking up new recipes to try out and was very happy.

Toby had won prizes for his floral displays and freshly grown vegetables that grew to an enormous size. He looked well and happy and had employed a new gardener to help with all the extra work and, Scruff was never very far away.

The handsome young gardener had lived in a one bedroom apartment some distance away and could barely afford the rent. He had been desperately searching for somewhere more suitable to live and had been over the moon when, Meg and Charlie had offered him the coach house at a peppercorn rent as long as he took care of it. He was delighted and promptly moved in. He had fallen head over heels in love with Sunbeam and they were often seen chatting together and holding hands.

Theo strutted about dressed as a pirate to the visitor's amazement. He regaled stories to delighted children that made their hair stand on end. The cave was a magical place and a favourite with everyone, and the play house was always busy with children dressing up and pretending to be pirates. He could be heard whistling a merry tune when he was alone.

Pearl was often seen pushing, Gabriel around the park

in his pram. Charlie was in charge of the boating lake that was very popular with everyone. Meg was always busy and, Sunbeam had taught her how to cook some mouth watering recipes, and Charlie was delighted.

Meg knew that her first vision of greenery and a beautiful landscape had been of, The Manor Park. She had many visions of the future which she wisely kept to herself. She is after all, a great psychic and in time will want to explore the world of ghosts.

END